Martin Faber: The Story of a Criminal

William Gilmore Simms

Table of Contents

Martin Faber: The Story of a Criminal

William Gilmore Simms

Kessinger Publishing reprints thousands of hard–to–find books!

Visit us at http://www.kessinger.net

`Since then, at an uncertain hour,

```
        That agony returns,
And, 'till my ghastly tale is told,
    This heart, within me, burns.'
```

Auncient Marinere.

Dedication

TO MY DAUGHTER— TO ONE, WHO, AS YET, CAN UNDERSTAND LITTLE
BUT HIS LOVE, THESE PAGES ARE FONDLY DEDICATED, WITH ALL THE
AFFECTIONS OF

A FATHER.

ADVERTISEMENT.

The work which follows is submitted with great deference and some doubt to the reader.
It is an experiment; and the style and spirit are, it is believed, something out of the beaten
track. The events are of real occurrence, and, to the judgment of the author, the
peculiarities of character which he has here drawn—if they may be considered such,
which are somewhat too common to human society— are genuine and unexaggerated.
The design of the work is purely moral, and the lessons sought to be inculcated are of
universal application and importance. They go to impress upon us the necessity of proper
and early education—they show the ready facility with which the best natural powers
may be perverted to the worst purposes—they stimulate to honorable deeds in the
young,—teach firmness under defeat and vicissitude, and hold forth a promise of ultimate
and complete success to well directed perseverance. By exhibiting, at the same time, the
injurious consequences directly flowing from each and every aberration from the
standard of a scrupulous morality, they enjoin the strictest and most jealous
conscientiousness. The character of Martin Faber, not less than that of William Harding,
may be found hourly in real life. The close observer may often meet with them. They are
here put in direct opposition, not less with the view to contrast and comparison, than
incident and interest. They will be found to develope, of themselves, and by their results,
the nature of the education which had been severally given them. When the author speaks
of education he does not so much refer to that received at the school and the academy. He

would be understood to indicate that which the young acquire at home in the parental dwelling—under the parental eye—in the domestic circle—at the family fireside, from those who, by nature, are best calculated to lay the guiding and the governing principles. It is not at the university that the affections and the moral faculties are to be tutored. The heart, and— *les petites morales*—the manners, have quite another school and other teachers, all of which are but too little considered by the guardians of the young. These are—the father and the mother and the friends—the play-mates and the play-places.

CHAPTER I.

"This is a fearful precipice, but I dare look upon it. What, indeed, may I not dare—what have I not dared! I look before me, and the prospect, to most men full of terrors, has few or none for me. Without adopting too greatly the spirit of cant which makes it a familiar phrase in the mouths of the many, death to me will prove a release from many strifes and terrors. I do not fear death. I look behind me, and though I may regret my crimes, they give me no compunctious apprehensions. They were among the occurrences known to, and a necessary sequence in the progress of time and the world's circumstance. They might have been committed by another as well as by myself. They must have been committed! I was but an instrument in the hands of a power with which I could not contend.

Yet, what a prospect, does this backward glance afford! How full of colors and characters— How variously dark and bright. I am dazzled and confounded at the various phases of my own life. I wonder at the prodigious strides which my own feet have taken— and as I live and must die, I am bold to declare,— in half the number of instances, without my own consciousness. Should I be considered the criminal, in deeds so committed? Had not my arm been impelled—had not my mood been prompted by powers and an agency apart from my own, I had not struck the blow. The demon was not of me, though presiding over, and prevailing within, me. Let those who may think, when the blood is boiling in their temples, analyze its throbs and the source of its impulses. I cannot. I am a fatalist. Enough for me that it was written!

My name is Martin Faber. I am of good family—of German extraction—the only son. I was born in M— village, and my parents were recognized as among the first in respectability and fortune of the place. The village was small—numbering some sixty families; and with a naturally strong and shrewd, and a somewhat improved mind, my father, Nicholas Faber, became the first man in it. The village of M—, was one of those that always keep stationary. The prospect was slight, therefore, of our family declining in influence. My father, on the contrary, grew every day stronger in the estimation of the people. He was their oracle—their counsellor— his word was law, and there were no rival pretensions set up in opposition to his supremacy. Would this had been less the case! Had Nicholas Faber been more his own, than the creature of others, Martin, his son, had not now obliterated all the good impressions of his family, and been called upon, not only to recount his disgrace and crime, but to pay its penalties. Had he bestowed more of his time in the regulation of his household, and less upon public affairs, the numberless vicious propensities, strikingly marked in me from childhood up, had, most probably been sufficiently restrained. But why speak of this? As I have already said—it was written!

The only child, I was necessarily a favorite. The pet of mama, the prodigy of papa, I was schooled to dogmatize and do as I pleased from my earlier infancy. I grew apace, but in compliance with maternal tenderness, which dreaded the too soon exposure of her child's nerves, health and sensibilities, I was withheld from school for sometime after other children are usually put in charge of a tutor. When sent, the case was not very greatly amended. I learned nothing, or what I learned was entirely obliterated by the nature of my education and treatment at home. I cared little to learn, and my tutor dared not coerce me. His name was Michael Andrews. He was a poor, miserable hireling, who having a large and depending family, dared not offend by the chastisement of the favorite son of a person of so much consequence as my father. Whatever I said or did, therefore, went by without notice, and with the most perfect impunity. I was a truant, and exulted in my irregularities, without the fear or prospect of punishment. I was brutal and boorish—savage and licentious. To inferiors I was wantonly cruel. In my connexion with superiors, I was cunning and hypocritical. If, wanting in physical strength, I dared not break ground and go to blows with my opponent, I, nevertheless, yielded not, except in appearance. I waited for my time, and seldom permitted the opportunity to escape, in which I could revenge myself with tenfold interest, for provocation or injustice. Nor did I discriminate between those to whom this conduct was exhibited. To all alike, I carried the same countenance. To the servant, the schoolmaster, the citizen, and even to my parents, I was rude and insolent. My defiance was ready for them all, and when, as sometimes, even at the most early stages of childhood, I passed beyond those bounds of toleration, assigned to my conduct, tacitly, as it were, by my father and mother, my only rebuke was in some such miserably unmeaning language as this—'Now, my dear—now Martin—how can you be so bad'—or, 'I will be vexed with you, Martin, if you go on so.'

What was such a rebuke to an overgrown boy, to whom continued and most unvarying deference, on all hands, had given the most extravagant idea of his own importance. I bade defiance to threats—I laughed at and scorned reproaches. I ridiculed the soothings and the entreaties of my mother; and her gifts and toys and favors, furnished in order to tempt me to the habits which she had not the courage to compel, were only received as things of course, which it was her duty to give me. My father, whose natural good sense, sometimes made him turn an eye of misgiving upon my practices, wanted the stern sense of duty which would probably have brought about a different habit; and when, as was occasionally the case, his words were harsh and his look austere, I went, muttering curses, from his presence, and howling back my defiance for his threats. I was thus brought up without a sense of propriety—without a feeling of fear. I had no respect for authority— no regard for morals. I was a brute from education, and whether nature did or not, contribute to the moral constitution of the creature which I now appear, certain, I am, that the course of tutorship which I received from all around me, would have made me so. You will argue from this against my notion of the destinies, since I admit, impliedly, that a different course of education, would have brought about different results. I think not. The case is still the same. I was fated to be so tutored.

CHAPTER II.

There was at the school to which I went, a boy about twelve, the same age with myself. His name was William Harding—he was the only child of a widow lady, living a retired life—of blameless character, and a disposition the most amiable and shrinking. This disposition was inherited by her son, in the most extravagant degree. He had been the child of affliction. His father had been murdered in a night affray in a neighbouring city, and his body had been brought home to the house and presence of his lady, when she was far advanced in pregnancy. The sudden and terrible character of the shock brought on the pains of labour. Her life was saved with difficulty, and, seemingly by miraculous interposition, the life of her infant was also preserved. But he was the creature of the deepest sensibility. His nervous organization was peculiarly susceptible. He was affected by circumstances the most trifling and casual—trembled and shrunk from every unwonted breeze— withered beneath reproach, and pined under neglect. So marked a character, presenting too, as it did, a contrast, so strikingly with my own, attracted my attention, at an early period of our school association. His dependence, his weakness, his terrors—all made him an object of a consideration which no other character would have provoked. I loved him—strange to say—and with a feeling of singular power. I fought his battles—I never permitted him to be imposed upon:—and he—could he do less?— he assisted me in my lessons, he worked my sums, he helped my understanding in its deficiencies, he reproved my improprieties—and I—I bore with and submitted patiently on most occasions to his reproofs. William Harding was a genius, and one of the first order; but his nervous susceptibilities left him perfectly hopeless and helpless. Collision with the world of man would have destroyed him; and, as it was, the excess of the imaginative quality which seemed to keep even pace with his sensibilities, left him continually struggling—and as continually to the injury and overthrow of the latter—with the calm suggestions of his judgment. He was a creature to be loved and pitied; and without entertaining, at this period, a single sentiment savoring of either of these, for any other existing being, I both loved and pitied him.

One day, to the surprize of all, William Harding appeared in his class, perfectly ignorant of his lesson. The master did not punish him with stripes, but, as the school was about to be dismissed, commanding the trembling boy before him, he hung about his neck a badge made of card, on which was conspicuously printed, the word `idler.'—With this badge he was required to return home, re–appearing at school with it the ensuing afternoon.

A more bitter disgrace could not, by any ingenuity, have been put upon the proud and delicate spirit of this ambitious boy. I never saw dismay more perfectly depicted upon any countenance. His spirit did not permit him to implore. But his eye—it spoke volumes of appeal—it was full of entreaty. The old man saw it not. The school was dismissed, and, in a paroxysm of grief which seemed to prostrate every faculty, my companion threw himself upon the long grass in the neighbourhood of the school–house, and refused to be comforted. I sought him out, and curious to know the cause of an omission which in him was remarkable, and should therefore have been overlooked by our tutor, I enquired of him the reason. The cruelty of his punishment was now more than ever, apparent to my eyes. His mother had been ill during the whole previous night, and he had been keeping watch and attending upon her. I was indignant, and urged him to throw aside the card beneath the trees, and resume it upon his return to the school. But he would not descend to the meanness of such an act, and resolutely determined to bear his punishment. I was of a different temper. Grown bold and confident by the frequent indulgencies which had so often sanctioned my own aberrations, I had already assumed the burdens of my comrades, escaping myself, while effecting their escape. Should I now hesitate, when a sense of justice, and a feeling of friendly sympathy coalesced towards the same end, both calling upon me for action. I did not. I seized upon the accursed tablet. I tore it from his bosom, and hacking it to pieces of the smallest dimensions, I hurled them to the winds, declaring, at the same time, his freedom, with a shout. He would have resisted, and honestly and earnestly endeavored to prevent the commission of the act. But in vain, and with a feeling of the truest satisfaction, I beheld him return home to his suffering parent. But my turn was to come. I had no fears for the consequence, having been accustomed to violate the rules of school, with impunity. Harding appearing without his badge, was questioned, and firmly refused to answer. I boldly pronounced my handiwork, no one else venturing to speak, fearing my vengeance, though several in the school, had been cognizant of the whole affair. At the usual hour of dismissal, I was instructed to remain, and when all had departed, I was taken by the master, into a small adjoining apartment, in which he usually studied and kept his books, and which formed the passage way from his school–room to his dwelling–house. Here I was conducted, and wondering and curious, at these preliminaries, here I awaited his presence. I had been guilty of insubordination and insurrection, and was not altogether sure that he would not proceed to flog me. But not so. He spoke to me like a father—as my father had never spoken to me— his words were those of monitorial kindness and regard. He described the evil consequences to his authority if such conduct were tolerated; and contented himself with requiring from me a promise of apology before the assembled school on the ensuing morning. I laughed in his face. He was indignant, as well he might be, and, under the momentary impulse, he gave me a smart blow with his open hand upon my cheek. I was but a boy— some thirteen or fourteen years of age,—but, at that moment, I measured with my eye the entire man before me, and though swelling with fury, coolly calculated the chances of success in a physical struggle. Had there been a stick or weapon, of any description at hand, I might not have hesitated. As it was, however, prudence came to my counsel. I submitted, though my heart rankled, and my spirit burned within me for revenge;—and I had it—years afterwards I had it—a deep, a dreadful revenge. For the time, however, I contented myself with one more congenial with the little spirit of a bad and brutal boy. In school–boy phrase, he kept me in—he took from me my freedom, locking me up safely in the little study, into which I had been conducted.

While in that room shut up, what were my emotions! The spirit of a demon was working within me, and the passions acting upon my spirit nearly exhausted my body. I threw myself upon the floor, and wept—hot, scalding and bitter tears. I stamped, I raved, I swore. On a sudden I heard the voice of Harding mournfully addressing me through the partition which separated the school room from my dungeon. He had come to sympathize, and, if possible, to assist me. But I would not know—I would not hear him. The gloomy frend was uppermost, and I suddenly became silent. I would not answer his inquiries—I was dumb to all his friendly appeals. In vain did the affectionate boy try every mode of winning me to hear and to reply. I was stubborn, and, at length, as the dusk came on, I could hear his departing footsteps, as he had slowly and sorrowfully given up his object in despair. He was gone, and I rose from the floor, upon which I had thrown myself. The first paroxysms of my anger had gone off, and their subdued expression gave me an opportunity more deeply to investigate my injuries, and meditate my revenge. I strode up and down the apartment for sometime, when, all of a sudden, I beheld the two large, new and beautiful globes, which my teacher had but a little while before purchased at a large price, and not without great difficulty, from his little savings. He was a philosopher, and this study was one of his greatest delights. My revenge stood embodied before me. I felt that I too could now administer pain and punishment. Though small in proportion to what, it appeared to me, my wrongs required, I well knew that to injure his globes, would be almost the severest injury I could inflict upon their owner. I did not pause—the demon was impatient. I seized the jug of ink that stood upon the shelf below them, and carefully poured its contents upon the beautifully varnished and colored outlines of the celestial regions. They were ruined—irreparably ruined; and where the ink, in its course, had failed to obliterate the figures, I took care that the omission should be amended by employing a feather, still further to complete their destruction. This, you may say, is quite too trifling an incident for record. No such thing. "The child's the parent of the man." In one sense, the life of the child is made up of trifles; but the exercises of his juvenile years will at all times indicate what they will be when he becomes old. The same passions which prompted the act just narrated, would move the grown incendiary to the firing of his neighbor's dwelling. The same passions prompted me in after years to exaggerated offences. How could it be otherwise? They were my fate!

Vainly would I endeavor to describe the rage, the agony of wrath, which came over the face of my tutor upon discovering what I had done. It is fresh in my memory, as if the occurrence had taken place but yesterday. I was in the study, where he had left me, upon his return. Indeed, I could not effect my escape, or I had certainly done so. The room was dark, and for some time, walking to and fro, and exhorting me in the most parental manner as he walked, he failed to perceive his globes or the injury they had sustained. In this way, he went on, speaking to me, in a way, which, had not my spirit been acted on by the arch enemy of man, must have had the effect of compelling me to acknowledge and to atone, by the only mode in my power, for my errors and misconduct. I had, indeed, begun to be touched. I felt a disposition to regret my act, and almost inclined to submission and apology. But on a sudden, he paused—the globes caught his eye—he approached and inspected them narrowly. Passing his hands over his eyes, he seemed to doubt the correctness of his vision; but when he ascertained, for a truth, the extent of the evil, tears actually started from the decaying orbs, and rolled as freely as from the eyes of childhood, down his lean and wrinkled face. Then was my triumph. I gloated in his suffering, and, actually, under the most involuntary impulse, I approached, and keenly watched his suffering. He beheld my approach—he saw the demon look of exultation which I wore; and human passion triumphed. He turned shortly upon me, and with a severe blow of his fist, he smote me to the ground. I was half stunned, but soon recovered, and with a degree of unconsciousness, perfectly brutish, I rushed upon him. But he was too much for me. He held me firmly with one hand, and, his anger now more fully provoked by my attack, he inflicted upon me a very severe flogging—almost the only one which I had ever received. It was certainly most richly deserved; but I thought not so then. I looked upon myself as the victim of a most unjustifiable—a most wanton persecution. I did not, for a moment, consider the vast robbery I had made from that poor old man's small stock of happiness and enjoyment. My feelings were all concentrated in self; and my ideas of justice, where my own interests or emotions were concerned, were in no degree abstract. I knew but one being in the world, whose claims were to be considered, and that individual, was, of course, myself.

I was now dismissed, and sore and smarting in body and mind, I returned to my home. I showed my bruises; I fabricated a story of greater wrongs and injuries. I dwelt upon the unprovoked aggression; taking care to suppress all particulars which might have modified the offence of my teacher. The flogging he had given me, had been a most severe one—and, the cause not being heard, would seem to have been most brutal. This was another part of my revenge, and it had its consequences. A solemn convocation of the chief men of the village, of whom my father was the dictator, incensed at the indignity, as it met their senses, and relying upon my *ex parte* representation, determined, without further hearing, upon the offence. Michael Andrews lost his school with every circumstance of ignominy; and in a most pitiable condition of poverty, in a few weeks, was compelled to leave the place. I was yet unsatisfied—my revenge was not altogether complete—boy as I was—unless I could actually survey it. I went to see him depart. I watched him, as in a miserable wagon, containing all his household gear, he drove into the adjacent country, attended by a wife and four young children. I exulted in the prospect; as, from a little hillock which overlooked the road they were compelled to travel, I looked down upon their departure. They beheld me, and the faces of all were immediately turned away. There is a dignified something in decent sorrow, and suffering borne in silence, which places it above, while it forbids anything like the spoken taunt or triumph;—I had otherwise shouted my cry of victory in their ears. As it was, they proceeded on their way into the country. I was, at length, satisfied with my revenge, and did not care to follow them.

CHAPTER III.

Under the direction of a more supple tutor than the first, I finished my education, if so we may call it. William Harding was still my associate. He was still the same nervous, susceptible, gentle youth; and though, as he grew older, the more yielding points of his character became modified in his associations with society, he nevertheless did not vary in his mental and moral make, from what I have already described him. Though disapproving of many of my habits and propensities, and continually exhorting me upon them, he yet felt the compliment which my spirit, involuntarily, as it were, rendered to his; and he was not at any time averse to the association which I tendered him. Still he was like me in few respects, if any. It is the somewhat popular notion that sympathy in pursuit, and opinions and sentiments in common, bring about the connexions of friendship and love. I think differently. Such connexions spring from a thousand causes which have no origin in mutual sympathies. The true source of the relationship is the dependence and weakness on the one hand—the strength and protection on the other. This, I verily believe, was the fact in our case.

With little other society than that of William Harding, years glided away, and if they brought little improvement to my moral attributes— they, at least, bringing no provocation, left in abeyance and dormancy, many of those which were decidedly immoral. My physical man was decidedly improved in their progress. My features underwent considerable change for the better—my manners were far less objectionable—I had suppressed the more rude and brutal features, and, mingling more with society—that particularly of the other sex—I had seen and obeyed the necessity of a gentlemanly demeanor. But my heart occupied the same place and character—there was no change in that region. There, all was stubborness and selfishness—a scorn for the possessions and claims of others—a resolute and persevering impulse which perpetually sought to exercise and elevate its own. The spell of my fate was upon it—it seemed seared and soured—and while it blighted, and sought to blight the fortunes and the feelings of others, without any sympathy, it seemed nevertheless, invariably, to partake of the blight. In this respect, in the vexation of my spirit at this strange inconsistency of character, I used to curse myself, that I was not like the serpent— that I could not envenom my enemy, without infecting my own system, with the poison meant only for his. To this mood, the want of employment gave activity if not exercise and exhibition. The secretions of my malignity, having no object of development, jaundiced my whole moral existence; and a general hostility to human nature and the things of society, at this stage of my being, vented itself in idle curses, and bitter but futile denunciations. I lived only in the night time—my life has been a long night, in which there has been no starlight— in which there have been many tempests. Talk not of Greenland darkness, or Norwegian ice. The moral darkness is the most solid—and what cold is there like that, where, walled in a black dungeon of hates and fears and sleepless hostility, the heart broods in bitterness and solitude, over its own cankering and malignant purposes.

Many years had now elapsed since my adventure with Michael Andrews, my old school–master. I had grown up to manhood, and my personal appearance, had been so completely changed by the forming hand of time, that I had not the same looks which distinguished me at that period. One morning, pursuing a favorite amusement, I had wandered with my gun for some distance, into a part of the country, which was almost entirely unknown to me. The game, though plentiful, was rather shy, and in its pursuit, I was easily seduced to a greater distance from our village, and on the opposite side of a stream, which though not a river, was yet sufficiently large, particularly when swollen by freshets,—a not unfrequent event—to make something like a barrier and dividing line between two divisions of the country. The day was fine, and without being at all conscious of the extent of my wanderings, I proceeded some fourteen or fifteen miles. My way led through a close and umbrageous forest. A grove of dwarf or scrub oaks, woven about with thick vines and sheltering foliage, gave a delightful air of quietness to the scene, which could not fail altogether in its effect on a spirit as discontented and querulous even as mine. Wandering from place to place in the silent and seemingly sacred haunt of the dreamy nature, I perceived, for the first time, a clear and beautifully winding creek, that stole in and out, half sheltered by the shrubbery growing thickly about it— now narrowing into a thin stream, and almost lost among the leaves, and now

11

spreading itself out in all the rippling and glassy beauty of a sylvan and secluded lake. I was won with its charms, and pursued it in all its bendings. The whole scene was unique in loveliness. The hum of the unquiet breeze, now resting among, and now flying from the slowly waving branches above, alone broke, at intervals, the solemn and mysterious repose of that silence, which here seemed to have taken up its exclusive abode. Upon a bank that jutted so far into the lake by a winding approach, as almost to seem an island, the trees had been taught to form themselves into a bower; while the grass, neatly trimmed within the enclosure, indicated the exercise of that art, whose hand has given life to the rock, and beauty to the wilderness. I was naturally attracted by the prospect, and approaching it from the point most sheltered, came suddenly into the presence of a tall and beautiful girl, about fifteen years of age, sitting within its shade, whose eyes cast down upon some needlework which she had in her hands, enabled me to survey, for sometime before she became conscious of my presence, the almost singular loveliness of feature and person which she possessed. She started, and trembled with a childish timidity at my approach, which not a little enhanced the charm of her beauty in my eyes. I apologized for my intrusion; made some commonplace inquiry and remark, and we soon grew familiar. The cottage in which her parents resided, was but a little way off, and I was permitted to attend her home. What was my surprize to discover in the person of her father, my old tutor. But, fortunately for me, he was not in a condition to recognize me. His mind and memory were in great part gone. He still contrived, mechanically as it were, to teach the `accidence' to three white–headed urchins, belonging to the neighborhood, and in this way, with the industry of his daughters, the family procured a tolerable livelihood. I was treated kindly by the old people, and had certainly made some slight impression on Emily—the maiden I had accompanied. I lingered for some hours in her company—and, though timid, uneducated and girlish in a great degree, I was fascinated by her beauty, her gentleness, and the angelic smile upon her lips.

It was late in the day when I left the house of old Andrews. He had heard my name, and showed no emotion. He had evidently forgotten all the circumstances of my boyhood in connexion with himself. I could then venture to return—to repeat my visits—to see once more, and when I pleased, the sweet object, whose glance had aroused in my bosom an emotion of sense and sentiment entirely unknown to it before. We did meet, and each returning day found me on the same route. Our intimacy increased, and she became my own—she was my victim.

CHAPTER IV.

That girl was the most artless—the most innocent of all God's creatures. Strange! that she should be condemned as a sacrifice to the wishes of the worst and wildest. But, it was her fate, not less than mine! Need I say that I—whose touch has cursed and contaminated all whose ill fortunes doomed them to any connexion with me—I blighted and blasted that innocence, and changed the smile into the tear, and the hope into the sorrow, of that fond and foolishly confiding creature. We were both, comparatively, children.—She was, indeed, in all respects a child—but I—I had lived years—many years of concentrated wickedness and crime. To do wrong was to be myself—it was natural. That I should deceive and dishonor, is not therefore matter of surprise; but that there should be no guardian angel—no protecting shield for the unwary and the innocent, would seem to manifest an unwise improvidence in the dispenser of things. A few months of our intimacy only had elapsed. In the quiet and secluded bower where we had first met, she lay in my arms. I had wrought her imagination to the utmost. With a stern sense and consciousness, all the while, of what I was doing, I had worked industriously upon the natural passions of her bosom. Her lips were breathing and burning beneath my own. Her bosom was beating violently against mine. My arm encircled and clasped her closely. There was a warm languor in the atmosphere—the trees murmured not— the winds were at repose—no warning voice rose in the woods—no tempest blackened in the sky—the shrill scream of a solitary bird at that moment might have broken the spell— might have saved the victim. But the scream came not—the fates had decreed it—body and soul, the victim was mine. She was no longer the pure, the glad, the innocent and unstained angel I had first known her. Her eyes were now downcast and fearful—her frame trembled with all the consciousness of guilt. She gave up all to her affection for one so worthless—so undeserving as myself: yet had she not my affections, though loving me, even as the young and morning flower may be seen to link and entwine itself with and about the deadly and venomous nightshade?

Our intercourse was continued in this way for several months. The consequences now began to threaten Emily with exposure, and she hourly besought me to provide against them by our marriage, as I had already frequently promised her to do. But I had no idea of making any such sacrifice. The passion which had prompted me at first, had no longer a place in my bosom. I did not any longer continue to deceive myself with the belief that she either was or could be any thing to me. She had few attractions now in my sight, and though still beautiful, more touchingly so, indeed, from an habitual sadness which her features had been taught to wear, than ever,—I had learned to be disgusted and to sicken at the frequency of her complaints, and the urgency and extravagance of her reproved none with me. I was not unwilling, for many reasons, that the marriage should take place. It will be sufficient to name one of these reasons. Though liberal, the allowance of money for my own expenditure, which I received from my father, had, for a long time past, been inadequate to the wants which my excesses necessarily occasioned. I had got largely into debt. I was harrassed by creditors; and had been compelled to resort to various improper expedients, to meet my exigencies. My more recent habits rendered a still further increase of stipend essential, for though, for some months, I had given my time chiefly to Emily, I had not yet so entirely divested myself of my old associates as to do with less money. My pride too, would not permit her to want for many things, and I had contributed, not a little towards the improvement of the condition of her family. It is well perhaps, that, in a chronicle of crime, almost unvarying, I should not altogether overlook those instances of conduct, which, if not praiseworthy, were, at least, not criminal. The marriage was therefore determined upon. Constance was an obedient child, and, without an affection existing, she consented to become my wife. Still, though making up my determination, without scruple on the subject, I confess I was not altogether at ease when my thoughts reverted to the condition of the poor girl I had dishonored. But what was that condition. In pecuniary matters, I could make her better off than ever—and, so far as caste was concerned— she could suffer no loss, for she had known no society. I never thought of the intrinsic value and necessity of virtue. My considerations were all selfish, and tributary to conventional estimates. With regard to our connexion, I saw no difficulty in marrying the heiress, and still enjoying, as before, the society of Emily. Matrimonial fidelity was still less a subject of concern; and, adjusting, in this way, the business and relations of the future, I hurried the arrangements and prepared assiduously for the enjoyments of the bridal.

CHAPTER V.

A sense of caution—or it may be of shame— determined me to keep the marriage, as long as I well could, from the knowledge of the one being whom it most injured. A few days before that assigned for the event, I proceeded to the place of usual rendezvous. I had not seen her for several days before; and her looks indicated sickness and suspicion. The latter appearance, I did not seem to observe, but her indisposition called forth my enquiries and regrets. I still strove to wear the guise of affection, but my words were cold, and my manner, I feel assured, wore all the features of the most confirmed indifference. "You look unwell, Emily," I observed, putting my arms around her—"you have not been so, have you?"

"Can you ask," was her reply, as her eyes were mournfully riveted upon my own; "could I continue well, and not see you for three days? alas! Martin, you little know how long a period in time is three whole days to me in your absence. Where have you been— have you been sick—you look not as you are wont to look. You are troubled and something afflicts you."

Her manner was tender in the extreme— the suggestion even by herself of indisposition as a cause of my absence, seemed to awaken all her solicitude, and to make her regret her own implied reproaches.

"I have been slightly unwell, Emily," was my reply, in a tone gravely adapted to indicate something of continued indisposition; and the possibility that this was the case, brought out all her fondness. How like a child—a sweet confiding child she then spoke to me. With what deep and fervid devotion—and, yet, at the very moment that the accents of her voice were most touching and tender, I had begun to hate her. She was in my way— I saw how utterly impossible it was, that, feeling for me as she did, she could ever tolerate a connexion with me, shared at the same time with another.

"But—there is one thing, Martin—one thing of which I would speak—and, hear me patiently, and be not angry, if in what I say, I may do you injustice and may not have heard rightly. Say, now, that you will not be angry with your Emily—that you will forgive her speech if it seem to call in question your integrity, for, as I live, Martin, I think you intend me no wrong."

And as she spoke, her hand grasped my arm convulsively, while one of her own, as if with a spasmodic effort, wound itself about my neck. I saw that the time for stern collision was at hand—that busy tongues had been about her, and I steeled myself stubbornly for the struggle and the strife.

"And, what do they say, Emily—and who are they that say, that which calls for such a note of preparation? Speak out—say on!"

15

"I will, Martin—but look not so upon me. I cannot bear your frown—any thing but that."

"Now then—what is said. What would you have, Emily?"

"There have been those to my mother, Martin—who have doubted your love for me, and, ignorant of how much importance it is to me now, who say, you are only seeking to beguile and to mislead me."

"They do me wrong, Emily—they speak false, believe me, as I live."

"I knew it, Martin—I knew that they did you wrong, and I told them so, but they sneered and laughed, and so they left me. But, Martin—they will speak to others, when I shall not be there to defend you, and we shall both suffer under their suspicions."

She paused here, and her eye sunk under the penetrating gaze of mine, but suddenly recovering, and hurrying herself, as if she feared the loss of that momentary impulse which then came to sustain her—she proceeded—

"I knew that I should suffer from you no injustice—I could not think it possible that you could wrong the poor girl, who had confided to you so far;—but Martin—do not smile at my folly—a something whispers me I have not long, not very long, to live, and I would be your wife—your married wife—before the time comes when my sin shall stand embodied before me. Let me have the *peace*—the *peace,* Martin, which our lawful union will bring with it; for now I have none. You have promised me frequently—say now that we shall be married this week—say on Thursday, Martin—on Thursday next that it shall take place."

I started as she concluded the sentence, as if I had been stung with an adder. Thursday was the day appointed for my marriage with Constance. Had she heard of this. I fixed my eyes attentively and searchingly upon her own; but though filled with tears, they quailed not beneath my glance. On the contrary her gaze was full of intenseness and expression. They conveyed, in dumb language the touching appeal of her subdued and apprehensive, though seemingly confident and assured, spirit. Disappointment, and the hope deferred that maketh the heart sick, had worn her into meagreness. Her cheeks were pale— her look was that of suppressed wretchedness, but these things touched me not. I had no notion of compliance, and my only thought was how to break off a connexion that

16

promised to be so excessively troublesome. I had now become completely tired of her, and told her peremptorily that it was impossible, for a variety of reasons, to grant her request. She implored—she made a thousand appeals to every supposed impulse and emotion of manhood and affection; to my pride, to my honor, to my love. I was inflexible; and finally, when she continued to press the matter with a warmth and earnestness natural to one in her situation, particularly as I had given no reason for my refusal, I grew brutally stern in my replies. I repulsed her tendernesses, and peevishly at length, uttered some threat, I know not what— of absence, or indifference, or anger.

She retreated from me a pace, and drawing her hands over her eyes, seemed desirous of shutting out the presence of a character so entirely new and unexpected, as I now appeared to her. For a moment she preserved this attitude in silence—then suddenly again approaching, in subdued accents, she spoke as at first.

"Your words and look, Martin, just now were so strange and unnatural that I was almost afraid of you. Do not speak so again to your Emily, but oh, grant her prayer—her last prayer. I do not pray for myself, for though I could not live without your affections, I shall not need them long, but I pray you to give a name, an honorable name, to the little innocent of this most precious burthen. Let it not, if it lives, curse the mother for the boon of a life which its fellows must despise, and speak of with scorn and ignominy."

I stood even this appeal. My heart was steeled within me, and, though I spoke to her less harshly, I spoke as hypocritically as ever. She saw through the thin veil which I had deemed it necessary to throw over my dishonesty, and a new expression took the place of tenderness in her features.

"It is all true then, as they have said," she exclaimed passionately. "Now, O God, do I feel my infirmity—now do I know my sin. And this is the creature I have loved—this is the thing—wanting in the heart to feel, and mean enough in soul to utter falsehood and prevaricate—this is the creature for whom I have sacrificed my heart—for whom I have given up, hopelessly and haplessly, my own soul. Oh, wretched fool—oh, miserable, most miserable folly. Yet think not," and as she turned upon me, she looked like the Priestess upon the tripod, influenced with inspiration— "Think not, mean traitor, as thou art—think not to triumph in thy farther seduction. Me thou hast destroyed,—I am thy victim, and I feel the doom already. But thou shalt go no farther in thy way. I will seek out this lady, for whose more attractive person, mine and my honor and affections, alike, are to be sacrificed. She shall hear from me all the truth. She shall know whether it be compatible with her honor and happiness, or the dignity of her character, to unite herself, in such bonds with a man who has proved so deadly, so dishonorable to her sex. And, oh, God"— she exclaimed, sinking fervently on her knee— "if it shall so happen that I save one such as I, from such a folly as mine, may it not expiate in thy sight, some portion of the sad offence of which I have been guilty."

She rose firmly and without a tear. Her eyes were red, her cheeks were burning with the fever of her whole frame, and she seemed, in all respects, the embodiment of a divine, a glorious inspiration. I was awed—I was alarmed. I had never before seen her exhibit any thing like daring or firmness of purpose. She was now the striking personification of both. She approached and sought to pass by me. I seized her hand. She withdrew it quickly and indignantly.

"Begone" she exclaimed—"I scorn, I despise you. Think not to keep me back. You have brought death and shame among my people in devoting me to both. You shall pollute me no more. Nay, speak not. No more falsehood, no more falsehood, for your own soul's sake. I would not that you should seem meaner in my sight, than you already are."

I seized her hand, and retained it by a fierce grasp.—

"Emily," I exclaimed, "what would you do— why is this? I ask but for delay, give me but a month, and all will be well—you shall then have what you ask—you shall then be satisfied."

"False—false! These assurances, sir, deceive me not now—they deceive me no more. My hope is gone, forever gone, that you will do me justice. I see through your hypocrisy— I know all your villainy, and Constance Claiborne shall know it too. Ha! do you start when her name is but mentioned. Think you, I know it not all—know I not that you have been bought with money—that, vile and mercenary as you are, you have not only sold me, and this unborn pledge of your dishonesty and my dishonor, but you have sold yourself. Seek not to keep me back. She shall hear it all from these lips, that thenceafter shall forever more be silent."

She struggled to free herself from my grasp, and endeavored to pass by me, with a desperate effort—her strength was opposed to mine, and in the heat of the struggle I forgot that victory in such a contest would be the heaviest shame. Yet, I only sought, at first, to arrest her progress. As I live, I had then no other object beyond. I certainly did not intend violence, far less further crime. But the fate was upon me;—she persisted in her design, and in the effort to prevent her passage, I hurled her to the ground. I paused, in a deadly stupor, after this. I was no longer a reasoning—a conscious being. She looked up to me imploringly—the desperate feeling which heretofore had nerved and strengthened her, seemed utterly to have departed. The tears were in her eyes, and, at that moment, she would have obeyed as I commanded— she would have yielded to all my requisitions— she would have been my slave. She met no answering gentleness in my eyes, and with a choking and vain effort at speech, she turned her face despairingly upon the still dewy grass, and sobbed, as if the strings of her heart were breaking in unison with each convulsion of her breast. At that moment, I know not what demon possessed me. There was a dead—a more than customary silence in all things around me. I felt a fury within me— a clamorous anxiety about my heart—a gnawing something that would not sleep, and could not be silent; and, without a thought of what I was to do, or what had been done, I knelt down beside her. My eyes wandered wildly around the forest, but at length, invariably settled, in the end, upon her. There was an instinct in all this. She had the look of an enemy to the secret and impelling nature within me, and, without uttering a single word, my fingers with an infernal gripe, were upon her throat. She could not now doubt the desperate character of my design, yet did she not struggle—but her eyes, they spoke, and such a language! A chain which I myself had thrown about her neck—that neck all symetry and whiteness—was in my way. I sought, but vainly, to tear it apart with my hands, and could only do so—with my teeth. In stooping for this, she writhed her head round and lifted her lips to mine. I shrunk, as from the fang of a serpent. They had a worse sting, at that moment, in my eyes. Mournfully, as she saw this, she implored my mercy.—

"Spare, forgive, dearest Martin, I will never vex you again—spare me this time, and I will be silent. Kill me not—kill me not"—more wildly she exclaimed as my grasp became more painful—"I am too young to die—I am too bad to perish in my sins. Spare me—spare me. I will not accuse you—I—God! Oh, God!"—and she was dead—dead beneath my hands!

CHAPTER VI.

I breathed not—I lived not for a minute. My senses were gone—my eyes were in the air, in the water, in the woods, but I dared not turn them, for an instant, to the still imploring glance of that now fixed and terrifying look of appeal. Still it pursued me, and I was forced to see—it was impossible that I could turn from the horrible expression—the dreadful glare, which shot from them through every muscle of my frame. The trees were hung with eyes that depended from them like leaves. Eyes looked at me from the water that gushed by us; and, as in a night of many stars, the heavens seemed clustering with gazing thousands, all bent down terrifically upon me. I started to my feet in desperation; and by a stern impulse I could not withstand, I pronounced audibly the name of my crime.

"Murder!"

Ten thousand echoes gave me back the sound. Tongues spoke it in every tree, and roused into something like demoniac defiance, I again shouted it back to them with the energies of a Stentor—then leaned eagerly forth to hear the replication. But this mood lasted not long. I was a murderer! I whispered it, as if in terror, to myself. I desired some assurance of the truth.

"I am a murderer!"

Spoken, however low, it still had its echo.

"Murderer!"—was the response of the trees, which had now tongues, as well as eyes. The agony grew intolerable, and a lethargic stupor came to my aid. I approached the corpse of my victim. Resolutely I approached it. How different was the aspect which her features now bore. She looked forth all her sweetness, and there was something—so I fancied—like forgiveness on her lips. Was it I that had defiled so pure an image—was it my hand, that, penetrating the sanctuary of life, had stolen the sacred fire from the altar? Oh, strange! that man should destroy the beauty which charms—the life that cheers and gladdens—the affection which won and nourishes him.

Deep in the centre of that forest stood an ancient rock. It was little known to the neighborhood, and its discouraging aspect and rude and difficult access had preserved it from frequent intrusion. I, however, whom no sterility could at any time deter, had explored its recesses, and it now suggested itself to my mind, as the place most calculated to keep the secret of my crime. A large natural cavity in one of its sides, difficult of approach, and inscrutable to research, seemed to present a natural tomb, and the suggestion was immediately seized upon. I took her in my arms—I pressed her to my heart— but in that pressure I maddened. I had not yet destroyed, in her death, the distinct principle of life which she carried within her. I felt the slight but certain motion of her child— of my child—struggling as it were for freedom. I closed my eyes—I suppressed the horrible thoughts which were crowding upon my brain, and hurrying on my way, sought out the cavity assigned for her repose. But a single plunge, and she was gone from sight, from reach. The rock was silent as the grave— it had no echoes—for, at that place and moment, I had no speech.

Will it be believed, the stride I had taken in crime, contributed largely to the sense of my own importance. I had never before doubted my capacity for evil—but I now felt—for I had realized—I had exercised—this capacity. There is something elevating—something attractive to the human brute, in being a destroyer. It was so with me. There was an increased vigor in my frame—there was new strength and elasticity in my tread—I feel assured that there was a loftier, a manlier expression in my look and manner. But, all was not so in my thought. There every thing was in uproar. There was a strange incoherence, an insane recklessness about my heart, where, if I may so phrase it, the spirit seemed prone to wandering about precipices and places of dread and danger. I kept continually repeating to myself, the name of my crime. I caught myself muttering over and over the word "Murder," and that, too, coupled with my own name. "Murderer," and "Martin Faber," seemed ever to my imagination the burden of a melody; and its music, laden with never ceasing echoes, heard by my own ears, was forever on my own lips.

CHAPTER VII.

I left the rock, slowly and frequently looking behind me. Sometimes my fancies confirmed to my sight the phantom of the murdered girl, issuing from the gaping aperture, and with waving arms, threatening and denouncing me. But I sternly put down these weak intruders. Though the first crime, of so deep a dye, which I had ever committed, I felt that the thoughts and feelings which came with the act, had been long familiar to my mind. The professional assassin could hardly look upon his last murder, with more composure, than I now surveyed the circumstances of my first. I was indeed a veteran, and in a past condition of society, I should have been a hero— the savior or the destroyer of a nation.

To be precipitate, was to be weak; so thought I even in that moment of fearful circumstances. I went back with all possible composure to the spot in which the crime had been committed. I examined the spot carefully— took with my eye the bearing and distances of all the surrounding objects in their connexion with the immediate spot on which the deed had been done. In this examination, I found the pocket handkerchief of Emily, with her name written in Indian ink upon it. I carefully cut it into shreds, dividing each particular letter, with my pen–knife, and distributing the several pieces at slow intervals upon the winds. Where our feet together had pressed the sands, with a handful of brush, I obliterated the traces; and in the performance of this task, I drew off my own shoes, leaving, only, as I proceeded, the impression of a naked foot. While thus engaged, I perceived for the first time, that I had lost a rich, and large cameo, from my bosom. The loss gave me no little concern, for, apart from the fact of its being generally known for mine, the intials of my name were engraven on the gold setting. How and where had it been lost. This was all important, and with indefatigable industry, I examined the grass and every spot of ground which I had gone over in the recent events. But in vain—it was not to be found, and with a feeling of uneasiness— not to describe my anxiety by a stronger epithet—I proceeded on my way home.

The poverty of Emily's family; the insulated position which they held in society; their inability to press an inquiry—were all so many safeguards and securities in my favor. There was some little stir, it is true—but I had so arranged matters that I passed unsuspected. The inquiry was confined to the particular part of country in which she resided—a lonely and almost uninhabited region—and, but a distant rumor of the crime reached our village— in which, the connexion existing between us was almost entirely unknown. The family had but few claims upon society, and but little interest was excited by their loss. In a little while all inquiry ceased; and with a random and general conclusion that she had fallen into the river, the thought of Emily Andrews gradually passed from the memories of those who had known her.

CHAPTER VIII.

The night came, appointed for my marriage with the beautiful and wealthy Constance Claiborne. Attended by William Harding, who, strange to say, in spite of the manifest and radical differences of character existing between us, was yet my principal companion, I was punctual to the hour of appointment. Every preparation had been made by which the ceremony should be attractive. A large company had been assembled. Lights in profusion— rich dresses—gayly dressed and decorated apartments, and the most various music, indicated the spirit of joy and perfect harmony with which our mutual families contemplated our union. I have already said, the bride was beautiful. Words cannot convey an idea of her beauty. She was emphatically a thing of light and love—

"Which seen, becomes a part of sight."

In grace, one knew not with what, save herself, to institute a comparison. In expression, there were volumes of romantic, and interesting poetry, embodied in each feature of her face; and the steel of my affections, stern as it was, wherever she turned, even as the dutiful needle to the pole, turned intuitively along with her. Such was the maiden,—so much after the make and mould of heaven, whom a cruel destiny was about to link with one formed in spirit after the fashion of hell.

The ceremony was begun. We stood up with linked hands at the altar. The priest went on with his formula. The bride's hand trembled in mine, and her eyes were commercing only with the richly carpeted floor. I was about to answer the question which should have made us one, when a cold wind seemed to encircle my body. My bones were numbed, and a freezing chill went through my whole system. My tongue refused its office, and, instinctively, as it were, bending to the opposite quarter of the apartment, my eyes fell upon a guest whom none had invited. There, palpable as when I had last seen her, stood the form of Emily Andrews. A pale and melancholy picture, and full of a terrible reproach. I was dumb, and for a moment, had eyes only for her. She was motionless, as when I had borne her to the unhallowed grave in which she did not rest. I felt that all eyes were upon me—the bride's hand was slowly withdrawn from mine, and that motion restored me. Mine were terrible energies. I seized her hand with a strong effort, and with a voice of the sternest emphasis, my eye firmly fixed upon the obtrusive phantom, I gave the required affirmative. With the word, the figure was gone.— I had conquered. You will tell me, as philosophers have long since told us, that this was all the work of imagination—a diseased and excited fancy, and in this you are probably right. But what of that? Is it less a matter of supernatural contrivance, that one's own spirit should be made to conjure up the spectres which haunt and harrow it, than that the dead should actually be made to embody themselves, as in life, for the same providence? The warning sound that chatters in my ear of approaching death may be, in fact, unuttered; but if my spirit, by an overruling fate, is calculated for the inception of such a sound, shall we hold it as less the work of a superior agency? Is it less an omen for that?

This was not all. At midnight, as I approached my chamber, the same ghastly spectre stood at the door as if to guard it against my entrance. For a moment I paused and faltered; but thought came to my relief. I knew that the energies of soul, immortal and from the highest as they are, were paramount, and I advanced. I stretched forth my hand to the key, and all was vacancy again before me. If my fancies conceived the ghost, my own energies were adequate to its control. In this I had achieved a new conquest, and my pride was proportionately increased and strengthened. I was thus taught how much was in my own power, in making even destiny subservient to my will!

CHAPTER IX.

I need not say that no happiness awaited me in my marriage. Still less is it necessary that I should tell you of the small amount of happiness that fell to the lot of my wife. I did not ill–treat her—that is to say, I employed neither blows nor violence; but I was a wretched discontent, and when I say this I have said all. She suffered with patience, however, and I sometimes found it impossible, and always difficult, to drive her beyond the boundary of yielding and forgiving humility. She loved me not from the first, and only became my bride from the absence of sufficient firmness of character, to resist the command. The discovery of this fact, which I soon made, offended my pride. I did not distrust, however—I hated her; and, with a strange perversity of character, which, let philosophers account for as they may—when I found that she could love, and that feelings were engendered in her bosom for another, hostile to her affection for me, though not at variance with her duties—I encouraged their growth. I nursed their developement. I stimulated their exercise; and strove, would you believe it, to make her the instrument of my own dishonor. But her sense of pride and propriety was greater than mine. Though conscious that her heart was another's, she unerringly held her faith to her husband, and my anger and dislike were exaggerated, when I discovered that my vice, even when allied to and assisted by her own feelings, could gain no ascendancy over her virtue.

She was won by the gentleness, the talent, the high character of my old friend, William Harding. She listened to his language with unreluctant and unconcealed pleasure. She delighted in his society; and with a feeling which she had never dared to name to herself, she gave him a preference, in every thought, in every emotion of her being. Nor—boy as he was—sensitive and easily wrought upon by respect and kindness—was he at all insensible to her regards. He became, as an acquaintance, almost an inmate of our house. He was always with us—and with the openness of heart common to such a character, he unreservedly sought for the society of Constance. I soon discovered their mutual propensities, for, at an early period, I had learned, with singular felicity, to analyze character. At first, and while she was yet a charming creation in my sight, and before I had learned to disregard and be indifferent to the admiration which she excited in others, this predilection gave me not a little concern. I was for a season the victim of a jealous doubt—not so much the result of a fear of offended honor, as of a weak pride and vanity, that was vexed at the preference given to him over myself, in the bosom of one, I strove to have exclusively my own. But this feeling went with the season. I grew indifferent at first, then pleased with their association, and finally it became an object with me, so to encourage it, as to give me a sufficient excuse and opportunity for a dreadful and overwhelming revenge. But they were both honest—honest as I had never been—as I never expected man or woman to have been! Twining and intermingling, hourly in spirit, the most jealous scrutiny, the most bitter hate and hostility, could never detect the slightest feature of impropriety in their conduct. Many were the modes which I chose to stimulate their passions—to influence their desires—to put their spirits into flame; and many were the opportunities with which I sought, in hurrying them to crime, to provide myself with victims. They went through the ordeal like angels—without one speck of earth; and pining with suppressed and strong affections, I beheld the cheek of Constance grow paler, day by day, and saw, at every visit—the increased wildness of look—the still exaggerated emotions struggling for utterance and life, in the bosom of the young and susceptible Harding.

CHAPTER X.

Some months had now elapsed since our marriage; and in this time, my house and young wife had lost most of their attractions. My favorite habit, and one which contributed not a little to my mood of sternness, was to take long walks into the neighboring country; and with my fowling–piece on my shoulder as apologetic for my idle wanderings, the neighboring forests for ten or fifteen miles round, soon became familiar to my survey. Sometimes, on these occasions, Harding would become my companion; and as he was highly contemplative in character, his presence did not at all interfere with the gloominess of my mood. It was on one of these occasions, while traversing a dense wood, thickly sown with undergrowth, and penetrable with difficulty, that we sat down together upon the trunk of a fallen tree, and fell into conversation. Our dialogue was prompted by the circumstances of our situation, and unconsciously I remarked—

"Harding, this is just such a spot, which one would choose in which to commit a murder!"

"Horrible!" was his reply, "what could put such a thought into your head? This, is just the spot now which I should choose for the inception of a divine poem. The awful stillness—the solemn gloom—the singular and sweet monotony of sound, coming from the breeze through the bending tree tops, all seem well calculated to beget fine thoughts,— daring fancies—bold and striking emotions."

"You talk of taking life, as if it were the crowning crime—it appears to me an error of society by which the existence of a being, limited to a duration of years, is invested with so much importance. A few years lopt from the life of an individual is certainly no such loss, shortening as it must, so many of his cares and troubles; and the true standard by which we should determine upon a deed, is the amount of good or evil which it may confer upon the person or persons immediately interested."

"That is not the standard," was his reply— "since that would be making a reference to varying and improper tribunals, to determine upon principles which should be even and immutable. But, even by such a standard, Martin, it would be a crime of the most horrible complexion, for, leave the choice to the one you seek to murder, and he will submit, in most cases, to the loss of all his worldly possessions, and even of his liberty, in preference to the loss of life."

"What would you say, William if you knew I had been guilty of this crime?"

"Say!" he exclaimed, as his eyes shot forth an expression of the deepest horror—"say!—I could say nothing—I could never look upon you again."

I looked at him with close attention for a moment, then, placing my hands upon his shoulder with a deliberation which was significant of the deepest madness, I spoke:

"Look—you shall look upon me again. I have been guilty of this same crime of taking life. I have been, and am, a murderer."

He sprung upon his feet with undisguised horror. His face was ashen pale—his lips were parted in affright; and while I held one of his hands, the other involuntarily was passed over, entirely concealing his eyes. What prompted me to the narration I know not. I could not resist the impulse—I was compelled to speak. It was my fate. I described my crime—I dwelt upon all its particulars; but with a caution, strangely inconsistent with the open confidence I had manifested, I changed the name of the victim—I varied the period, and falsified, in my narrative, all the localities of the crime; concluding with describing her place of burial beneath a tree, in a certain ground which was immediately contiguous, and well known to us both.

He heard me out with wonder and astonishment. His terror shook his frame as with an ague, and at the conclusion he tried to laugh, and his teeth chattered in the effort.

"It is but a story," he said chokingly, "a horrible story, Martin, and why do you tell it me? I almost thought it true from the earnest manner in which you narrated it."

"It is true, William—true as you now stand before me. You doubt, I will swear—"

"Oh, swear not—I would rather not believe you—say no more, I pray you—tell me no more."

With a studied desperation—a malignant pleasure, increasing in due proportion with the degree of mental torture which he appeared to undergo, I went again over the whole story as I had before told it—taking care that my description of each particular should be made as vivid as the solemn and bold truth certainly made it.

"I am a murderer! William Harding!"

"May God forgive you, Martin—but why have you told me this—would you murder me, Martin? Have I done any thing to offend you?"

His excessive nervousness, at length, grew painful, even to myself. "Nay, fear not, I would not harm you, William, for the world. I would rather serve and save you. But keep my secret—I have told it you in confidence, and you will not betray me."

"Horrible confidence!" was his only reply, as we took our way from the forest.

CHAPTER XI.

Several days had passed since this conference, and, contrary to his custom, Harding, in all this time, had kept out of my sight. His absence was felt by both Constance and myself. He had been, of late, almost the only companion known to either of us. Why I liked him I knew not. His virtues were many, and virtues were, at no time, a subject of my admiration. That he was loved by Constance, I had no question; that he loved her I felt equally certain—but it was the passion of an angel on the part of both; and it may be that knowing the torture which it brought with it to both of them, my malignant spirit found pleasure in bringing them together. It was not a charitable mood, I am satisfied, that made me solicitous that he should be as much as possible an inmate of my dwelling.

He came at last, and I was struck with his appearance. The change for the worse was dreadfully obvious. He looked like one, who had been for many nights without sleep. He was pale, nervous in the last degree, and awfully haggard.

"I am miserable," said he, "since you breathed that accursed story in my ears. Tell me, I conjure you, Martin, as you value my quiet, that you but jested with me—that the whole affair was but a fabrication—a fetch of the nightmare—a mere vision of the fancy."

Will it be believed, that having thus an opportunity, even then, of undoing the impression I had created, I took no advantage of it. I persisted in the story—I was impelled to do so, and could not forbear. There was an impulse that mastered the will—that defied the cooler judgment—that led me waywardly, as it thought proper. You have read that strange poem of Coleridge, in which the "Auncient Marinere" is made, whether he will or no, and in spite of every obstacle, to thrust his terrible narrative into the ears of the unwilling listener. It was so with me; but though I was thus compelled to denounce my crime, the will had still some exercise, and I made use of it for my security. I changed the particulars so materially from the facts, as they really were, that inquiry must only have resulted in my acquittal. The state of mind under which Harding labored, was of melancholy consequence, to him, at least, if not to me. Sad and disappointed, he left me without a word, and for some days more I saw him not. At length he came to me looking worse than ever.

"I shall go mad, Faber, with this infernal secret. It keeps me awake all night. It fills my chamber with spectres. I am haunted with the presence of the girl, you accuse yourself of having murdered.

"Go to—will you be a child all your life. Why should she haunt you?—it is not you who have murdered her—she does not trouble me.

"Nevertheless, she does. She calls upon me to bring you to justice. I awake and she is muttering in my ears. She implores—she threatens—she stands by my bed side in the darkness—she shakes the curtains—I hear the rustling of her garments—I hear her words; and when I seek to sleep, her cries of "Murder,! Murder! Murder!" are shouted, and ring through all my senses, as the sound of a sullen, swinging bell in the wilderness. Save me, Martin—from this vision—save me from the consequence of your own imprudence in telling me this story. Assure me that it is untrue, or I feel that I shall be unable to keep the secret. It is like a millstone around my neck—it makes a hell within my heart."

"What! and would you betray me—would you bring me to punishment, for an offence which I have told you was involuntary, and which I unconsciously committed? Your sense of honor, apart from your feeling of friendship, alone, should be sufficient to restrain you. I cannot believe that you would violate your pledge—that you can betray the confidence reposed in you."

Silenced, but not satisfied, and far more miserable than ever, the poor youth, whose nerves were daily become more and more unsteady and sensitive under these exciting influences, went away;—but the next day, he came again—his look was fixed and resolute, and an air of desperate decision marked every feature.

"I am about to go to the Justice, Martin, to reveal all this story, precisely as you have told it to me—I cannot bear a continuance of life, haunted as I have been, by innumerable terrors, ever since I heard it. But last night, I heard the distinct denunciations of the murdered girl, couched in the strongest language, emphatically uttered in my ears. The whole scene was before me, and the horrors of the damned, could not exceed those which encompassed my spirit. I fled from the chamber— from the house. In the woods I have passed the whole night in the deepest prayer. My determination is the result of the soundest conviction of its necessity. I can keep your secret no longer."

I paused for a moment, and having prepared myself for all difficulties by a consideration of all the circumstances, I simply bade him—"Go then—if he was determined upon the betrayal of his friend and the forfeiture of his honor."

"Reproach me not thus, Martin"—was his reply. "Forgive me, but I must do so. I must either disclose all or commit self–murder. I cannot keep within my bosom that which makes it an Ætna—which keeps it forever in flame and explosion. Forgive—forgive me!" Thus speaking, he rushed from my presence.

CHAPTER XII.

I was cited before the Justice, and the testimony of William Harding delivered with the most circumstantial minuteness, was taken down in my presence. Never did I see a more striking instance of conscience struggling with feeling—never had I conceived of so complete a conquest of one over the other. I denied all. I denied that I had ever made him such a statement—that we had ever had any such conversation; and with the coolness and composure of veteran crime, wondered at the marvellous insanity of his representations. He was dumb, he looked absolutely terrified. Of course, however, in such an examination, my own statements were unavailing; and his were to be sustained by a reference to the localities and such of the details which he had made, as might ostensibly contribute to its sustenance or overthrow. Search was made under the tree where my victim was alledged to have been buried. The earth appeared never to have been disturbed from the creation — upon digging, nothing was found. So, with all other particulars. Harding's representations were confuted. He was regarded by all as a malignant wretch, who envied the felicity, and sought to sting the hand of him who had cherished and befriended him. The public regard feel away from him, and he was universally avoided. I affected to consider him the victim of momentary hallucination, and the christian charity thus manifested, became the admiration of all. I almost dreaded that I should be deified— made a deacon in life, and a saint after death.

Poor Harding sunk silently to his den. Sensitively alive to public opinion, as well as private regard, his mind reeled to and fro, like a storm troubled vessel, beneath a shock so terrible and unexpected. He had lived upon the breath of fame—he was jealous of high reputation—he was tremblingly alive to those very regards of the multitude, which were now succeeded by their scorn and hisses. What a blow had I given him—but he was not yet to escape me. I suffered a day or two to elapse, and then sought him out in his chamber. I entered, and looked upon him for several minutes unobserved. His head was between his hands, and his chin rested upon the table. His air was that of the most woful *abandon*. The nature of his feelings might be inferred, along with his personal appearance, from the nature of the companions beside, and the general condition of things around him. One boot was thrown off, and lay upon the floor—the other, as if he had grown incapable of further effort, was permitted to remain upon his foot. The mirror lay in the smallest pieces about the room; the contemplation of his own features, blasted as they had been with the shame of his situation, having prompted him, as he came from the place of trial, to dash his hand through it. On the table, and on each side of him, lay— strangely associated—his bible and his pistols. He had been about to refer to one or to the other of them for consolation. It was in this situation, that I found him out. I brought increased tortures—while the people, who saw and wondered, gave me credit for christian benevolence. How many virtues would put on the most atrocious features, could their true motives be pursued through the hive of venomous purposes that so frequently swarm and occupy the secret cells and caverns of the human heart!

He saw me at length, and, as if the associations which my presence had called up, were too terrible for contemplation, he buried his head in his hands, and again thrust them on the table. As I approached, however, he started from this position—a mood entirely new, appeared to seize upon him, and snatching the pistol which lay before him upon the table, he rushed to meet me. He placed it upon my bosom, and deliberately cocked it, placing his finger at the same moment upon the trigger. A glare of hellish desperation, flowed out from his eyes, as with words that seemed rather shrieked than articulated, he exclaimed— " And what is there that keeps me from destroying you? What should stay my hand—what should interpose to protect you from my just revenge—what should keep you from the retributive wrath, which you have roused into fury?"

31

Martin Faber: The Story of a Criminal

I made no movement—precipitation, or any act or gesture, on my part, at that moment, would have been instant death. He would have felt his superiority. I maintained my position, and without raising a finger, I replied with the utmost deliberation:—

"What should keep you from taking my life! What a question! Would you be answered?— Your own fears.—You know that I would haunt you."

The pistol dropped from his hands, and he trembled all over. I proceeded.

"You should have no peace—no moment of repose secure from my intrusion—no single hour you should call your own. I should link myself to you, as Mezentius' dead, to his condemned and living victim. I would come between you and your dearest joys, nor depart for a solitary moment from a share in all the unavoidable duties and performances of life. We should sit, side by side, at the same table— sleep in the same couch,—dwell in the same dwelling. Would you rise to speak in the council, I should prompt your words—I should guide your action. Would you travel, I would mount the box and impel in the direction of my caprice. Would you love, I would figure in your courtship—go between yourself and mistress, and assist in your bridal. Your own wife should not have one half of the communion I should enjoy with you!"

He was paralyzed with his agony.

"Terrible man!" he exclaimed, "What would you do with me; why am I made your victim—why do you persecute me? I have not wronged; I have not sought to wrong you. You, on the contrary, have destroyed me, and yet would pursue me further. You have been my evil genius."

"I know it—I deplore it!"

"You deplore it! Horrible mockery! How shall I believe your speech after what has happened. Why deny the story, yourself poured into my ears as the truth."

"It was the truth!"

"Yet you swore it was false!"

Martin Faber: The Story of a Criminal

"Life is sweet—life is necessary, if not to human joys, at least, to the opportunities of human repentance. Would you have me give myself to an ignominious death upon the scaffold— disgracing my family, dishonoring myself, and dooming all who shared in my communion to a kindred dishonor with myself?"

"Why then did you tell me of this crime?"

"I could not help it. The impulse was native and involuntary, and I could not disobey it. It would not be resisted. It burned in my bosom as it has done in yours, and, until I had revealed it, I could hope for no relief."

"Dreadful alternative! Hear me, Martin Faber—hear me and pity me. You know my history—you know my hopes—my pretensions— my ambition. You know that for years, from my boyhood up, in despite of poverty, and the want of friends and relatives, I have been contending for glory—for a name. You know that the little world in which we live, had begun to be friendly to my aspirations— that they looked on my progress with sympathy and encouragement—that they pointed to me as one likely to do them honor— to confer a name upon my country as well as upon myself. You know that for years, in solitude, and throughout the long hours of the dark and wintery night, I have pursued my solitary toil for these objects. That I have shrunk from the society that has been wooing me—that I have denied myself all the enjoyments which are the life of other men—that I have, in short, been sacrificing the present for the future existence—the undying memory of greatness, which it had been my hope, to leave behind me. This you knew—this you know. In one hour, you—without an object—to satisfy a wanton caprice—you have overthrown all these hopes—you have made all these labors valueless—you have destroyed me. Those who loved, hate me—those who admired, contemn— those who praised, now curse and denounce me as a wanton and malicious enemy, seeking the destruction of my friend! I am not only an exile from my species—I am banished from that which has been the life–blood of my being—the possession of a goodly, of a mighty name! I have no further use in life."

"All is true—you have said but the truth. I am conscious of it all."

"Oh, speak not, I conjure you—I need not your assurances in my confirmation. I do not ask your voice. Hear me in what I shall say, and if you can, heal as far as you may heal, the wounds you have inflicted."

"Speak on!"

"I will seek to reconcile myself to the condition— to the exile to which you have driven me. I will struggle to give up the high hopes which have prompted and cheered me, through the unalleviated and unlighted labors of my life—I will struggle to be—nothing! All I ask is that you should give me peace—permit me to sleep once more. Say that you have not committed the crime, of which you have accused yourself. Give me this assurance, and free me from this gibbering and always present spectre, that, roused for ever by my fancies, refuses to be gone !"

How easy to have granted this request ! How impossible, indeed, would it appear, to have refused an appeal, urged under such circumstances. But I did refuse — I reiterated the story of my crime, as I had uttered it before, without any variation, and the nervously susceptible youth sunk down before me, in despair, upon the floor. In a moment, however, he arose, and — smile was upon his lips. There was a fearful energy in his eye, which had never marked it before, and which it surprised me not a little to survey. With a strong effort, he approached me.

"I will be no longer a child — I will shake off this fever of feeling which is destroying me.

I will conquer these fancies—I will not be their slave. Shall I possess a mind, so soaring and absolute, to bow down to the tyrant of my own imaginings? I will live for better things. I will make an effort!"

I applauded his determination, and persuaded him to go with me, as before, to my residence. This, though good policy with me, was the height of bad policy with him. The world looked upon me as the most forgiving and foolishly weak philanthropist—a benevolent creation of the very finest water. The readiness with which Harding again sought my hospitality, after his charges against me, was, of course, still further in evidence, against the honesty of his intentions. They looked upon his depravity as of the most heinous character, and numberless were the warnings which I hourly received, of the thousand stings which the—so–called—serpent was treasuring up for my bosom. But, I affected to think differently. I put all in his conduct down to a momentary aberration of intellect, and urged the beauty and propriety of christian forgiveness. Was I not of a most saint–like temper? They thought so.

CHAPTER XIII.

It is strange, that, with my extended and perfect knowledge of human character, and my great love of mental and moral analysis, I should have suffered myself to be taken in by these external shows on the part of my victim. Strange, that so sudden—so unlooked for, an alteration from his wonted habit had not aroused my jealousy—my suspicion of some hidden motive. But, my blindness was a part of my fate, or, how should it have been that a creature so weak, so utterly dependent as Harding had ever been, should have deceived a spirit so lynx−eyed as mine. Led to consider him too greatly the victim of the nervous irritability, boy which, indeed, his every action and impulse was distinguished, I had not looked for the exercise, in his mind, of any of that kind of energy, which would carry him undeviatingly and perseveringly to the attainment of any remote or difficult object, or to the accomplishment of a far and foreign purpose. I had neglected entirely to allow for the stimulating properties of a defeat, to a mind which had only lived for a single object. I had refused to count upon the decision of character, which, might, by probability, arise in a mind, however in all other respects, variable and vascillating, when concentrating itself upon the attainment of a single end, and that, too, of a kind, so absorbing, so all impelling as the attainment of fame. I did not recollect that Harding had himself acknowledged the existence of one only passion, in his bosom; or, I should have seen that his present change of manner, was but a thin veil disguising and concealing some ulterior project, subservient to the leading passion of his spirit. I failed, therefore,—fool that I was—to perceive the occult design, which of a sudden had so completely altered all the obvious characteristics of my companion—his habits, his temper, and his hopes. Folly to suppose, that with the loss of public estimation, he would be content with life unless with a desperate effort to regain his position. And how could he regain that position? How, but by establishing my guilt, and his innocence of all malevolent intention. And such was his design. Assured, as he now was, that I was in truth a criminal—that I had committed the murder of which I had accused myself, and that I had only so varied the statement of its particulars as to mislead and defeat enquiry— and looking forward to the one single object,— that of restoring himself to the popular regards of which I had deprived him—he was determined, of himself, to establish my crime— to trace the story from the very imperfect data I had myself given him, and by perpetual associations with myself, and a close examination into my moral make, to find out the materials of evidence which should substantiate his now defeated accusations. How blind was I not to have perceived his object—not to see through his unaccustomed artifices! The genius—the gigantic genius of his mind, will be best comprehended from this curious and great undertaking, and from the ingenuity and indefatigable industry with which he pursued it. Nor, from this fact, alone, but coupled, as under existing circumstances was the pursuit adopted, his strength of character and firmness of mind, are of the most wonderful description. The task was attended with an association, which, for a protracted period of time, still further exposed him to the scornful execrations and indignation of those, for whose good opinion, alone, he was voluntarily about to undergo all this additional load of obloquy. Under these aspects the effort was a highsouled and sublime one, and furnished one of the best proofs of the moral elevation of his genius. I regard it now, when too late to arrest its exercise and progress, with a sentiment little short of wonder and admiration.

All these occurrences, had, of course, been made known to my wife; and shocked and terrified as she had been—torn and distracted between a sense of duty to myself, and a feeling of deep, but unexpressed regard for my accuser—when, for the first time after the trial, I brought him to the house, with a highly proper spirit—seeing the affair as she had seen it—she declined making her appearance. I insisted upon it:—

"How can you require such a thing?" was her very natural inquiry. "Whatever may have been his motive, has he not sought your life. Has he not brought a foul and false accusation against you, making you a criminal of the darkest dye?"

"Look at me, Constance," I said in reply, as I took one of her hands in mine—"I am the criminal—I committed the crime he charged upon me, and which I myself had revealed to him. His accusation, so far as he was concerned, was neither foul nor false!"

And wherefore did I tell her this? Why should I have multiplied the evidence against me—why put myself at the mercy of another? It might be enough to say that I did not fear that Constance would betray me. As she was a pure and delicate woman, her love for him—treasured up in secret, and a source of trembling and self-reproach, as I knew it must be, to her heart—was my sufficient security. She would not have linked her testimony with his, however she might have hated me and loved him, fearing that her motives might be subject to the suspicion of others, as she herself would have suspected them. This consideration would have left me without fear, in that quarter, but this was not a consideration with me, in telling her the story. I could not refrain from telling it—in spite of myself I was compelled to do so—it was my fate.

I shall not attempt to describe her horror. She was dumb, and in silence descended with me to the apartment in which Harding had been left. To him this was a moment of fearful ordeal. The woman he loved, though hopelessly, he had struck, through her husband. He was not to know that I had most effectually acquitted him, to her, of the offence, for which he anticipated her scorn and hatred. His anxiety and wretchedness were again manifest until she relieved him, as with a boldness of spirit which I had never before seen her manifest, she walked forward, took his hand, and welcomed him as if nothing had happened. He looked first to me, then to her and silently, with a tearful eye, and frame violently agitated, he carried her hand to his lips. She retreated, and was deeply confused by this act. I saw her inmost soul, at that moment in her face. Why had she not loved me as she loved him? Why, oh, why?

That night, in my chamber, I said to her— "You love this youth—speak not—I would not have you deny it. I will tell you more— would you know it?—he loves you too, and there are few persons in the world more deserving the love of one another. Were I dead to–morrow you would most probably make the discovery, and—"

"Oh, Martin Faber, I see not why you should torment me in this manner. For heaven's sake, let me have peace. Make not all miserable about you; or, if you are bent on making me so, let not your malice exercise itself on this unhappy youth, whose life you have already embittered, whose prospects you have blighted—and to whom every hour of association with yourself, must work additional evil. Persuade him, for the repose of all, to leave the country."

"Would you fly with him! Beware, woman! Think not to deceive me—I see into your heart, and understand all its sinuosities. Look that your interest in this enthusiast gets not the better of your duty."

She turned her head upon the pillow, and sobbed bitterly:—yet, how wantonly had I uttered these reproaches. The angels were not more innocent in spirit than was she at that moment when I had inflicted upon her the tortures of the damned.

CHAPTER XIV.

I am now rather to narrate the labors of another than of myself, and to record the progress of Harding in the newly assumed duties of his life, of which, to their termination, I had little, if any suspicion.

In accordance with his design, and in this respect, my own habits and disposition favored him largely, he was with me at all hours—we were inseparable. He pretended a taste for gunning, and though a poor sportsman, provided with the usual accoutrements, he would sally forth with me, day after day, in the pursuit of the game, in which the neighboring country was plentifully supplied. Day by day, at all hours, in all places, we were still together, and seemingly in the same pursuit; yet, did we not always hunt. We chose fine rambles—pleasant and devious windings of country, secluded roads, hills and dales and deep forests, in which a moody and reflective spirit might well indulge in its favorite fancies. Of this make were we both. To–day we were in one direction—to–morrow in another, until the neighboring world and woods, for an extent in some quarters of twenty miles, became familiar to us in our excursions. I was struck with Harding's new habit of observation. In our rambles before he had seen, or appeared to see, nothing. Now nothing escaped his notice and attention. Tree and stump—hill and vale—wood and water—all grew familiar, and a subject of large and narrow examination. He seemed particularly solicitous of the true relations of things—of parallel distances—objects of comparative size, and the dependencies of a group, in the compass of his survey. Having great fondness for landscape drawing and some skill in the art, I put these peculiarities down to the account of this propensity, and gave myself no concern about it; but not unfrequently, turning suddenly, would I detect the fixed gaze of his eye, fastened inquiringly upon my own. On such occasions he would turn aside with a degree of confusion, which, did not, however, provoke my suspicions. There was no object in these wanderings that seemed too humble for his survey. He peered into every cup of the hills—into hollow trees—groped his way through the most thickly spread and seemingly impervious undergrowth, and suffered no fatigue, and shrunk back from no difficulty. Having hit upon a new spot, which looked impervious or dark, he would, before its examination, closely watch my progress— the direction which I took and the peculiar expression of my face. These practices were not unseen by me then, but I regarded them as having no object—I was certainly blind to their true one. It is only now that the mystery of his mind is unveiled—that his new–born daring is accounted for—that he now appears the rational and strong spirit I had not then regarded him.

We had now, in these rambles, taken, with the exception of a single one, every possible route, leading into the neighboring country. Bold and daring as I was, I had always avoided the path which led to the little islet and the scenes of my crime, though, certainly without exception, the most beautiful and attractive among them. This had not escaped his attention—though he had so contrived it, as not to appear to have a care or even to be conscious, what route we were to pursue. It now happened, however, that we were called upon to retread spots which had grown familiar, and more than once my companion would exclaim—

"Have we not been here before—can we not take some new direction?"

Still I avoided the route too well known to me, and still he had not ventured to propose taking it. He would not alarm me by a suggestion, though one which would have been so perfectly natural. He took another mode to effect his purpose, and one day, just as we were about to pass the little hollow in the woods, which led directly upon the path I so much wished to avoid, he saw, or pretended to see, some game upon which to exercise his skill, and, without saying more, he darted into the avenue. I was compelled to follow, and, slowly, and with feelings I was ashamed to possess, but could not control, I prepared to call up the whole history of crime and terror, already sufficiently vivid to the eye of memory. We pursued the devious route, and once more I found myself retracing a region, which though for months untrodden, was still as freshly in my recollections, as when I made it the field of exercise for all the black and blasting passions running then riot in my soul. On we went from point to point, of all the places in my memory, each of which had its distinct association, and spoke audibly to my spirit of some endearment or reproach, some sorrow or delight. Here was the little lake,—here the islet where I first discovered her. Here the scene of her dishonor and of my triumph— here the place of our usual meeting, and here— the spot upon which she perished under my hands. I strove not to look. I felt all things too vividly in my soul, and though I closed my eyes, I could not shut out the images of terror which were momentarily conjured up by my imagination. I strove to look in all quarters but in that which witnessed our struggle and my crime, but my eyes invariably turned at last and settled down on the one spot, where, I beheld, at length, the distinct outline of her figure, as it had, at the time, appeared before me. Slowly it seemed to rise from its recumbent posture, and, while I breathed not, I beheld it proceed along the road which I had taken, when bearing the inanimate burden from which that now guiding spirit had forever departed, to its place of final slumber in the body of the rock, which stood rigidly in the distance. I followed it, unconsciously, with my eyes. My respiration had utterly ceased—my hair was moist and active—my lips were colorless and cold, and my cheeks were ashen. A palsying wind seemed to penetrate my bones, and though not a joint trembled, yet they were all powerless. I became conscious at last of my condition and appearance, from discovering the eyes of Harding anxiously bent upon mine and following the direction of their gaze. There was something so expressive—so earnest in his look, that, though yet utterly unsuspicious of his design, I was nevertheless not a little offended at his seeming curiosity. I recovered myself on the instant of making this discovery, and turned round abruptly upon him. As if detected in some impropriety, his eyes fell from the look which I gave him in evident confusion; and, without a word, we prepared to proceed in our ramble. Not willing to suggest a solitary movement while in this region, which should prompt doubt or inquiry, I left the choice of road to himself, and saw with some concern that we were now taking the direct route to the cottage of old Andrews, the father of Emily. I had no fear of exposure from any such interview, for, I had so contrived it, that all suspicion was diverted from myself in the minds of the family. I had busied myself in the little inquiries that had been made into her fate—had pretended not a small portion of sorrow and regret—had made sundry presents, which in the depressed condition in which they lived, had readily contributed still more to their blindness; and never having been recognized, in the dotage of the old man, as the boy who had contributed to his first great misfortune, I had escaped all imputations on the subject of the second. Besides, I had taken care to visit them frequently, though privately, for a short period of time after the event, and felt secure that I had no other position in their regard, than that of confiding and friendly consideration. But the subject had become irksome, and, in addition to this fact, I had, for the first time, perceived in my mind the possibility that my companion, coupling the conversation of the family, which would most probably turn upon the fate of their daughter, with my own story, might be enabled to gather from the particulars such information as would open the trail, and prepare the way for further evidence. But the cautious policy of Harding silenced my alarm, and indeed, my great error from the first, consisted in the humble estimate I had been taught to make of his character for firmness. There is no greater mistake, than in despising him to whom you have given a reason to become an enemy. Where there is mind, contempt will engender malice, and where there is malice, there is a ceaseless prompter, which one day will couple the venom with the sting. Self-esteem in exaggerating my own strength to myself, had also taught me to undervalue that of others—in this way, I assisted his pursuit, and helped him to his object.

We came soon upon the cottage. The old man sat glowering in idiotic abstraction in a corner chair, which he kept in a continual rocking motion. His mind seemed utterly gone, and though he spoke to both, he appeared to recognize neither of us. His wife was glad to see me, and thanked me repeatedly for some articles of dress which I had sent her some months before, since which period, until then, I had not seen her. An unavoidable association called up the memory of Emily, and the tears of the old woman were again renewed. Harding with an air of common–place inquiry, and a manner of the most perfect indifference, almost amounting to unconsciousness, inquired into the story to which she had referred, and while she told it as far as it was known to herself, busied himself in plaiting into something like form, the remains of a handful of osiers which he had plucked on the way. His very indifference, had not my fate otherwise ordained, should have alarmed my watchfulness, so utterly different did it appear from the emotion which he usually expressed when called to listen to a narrative so sorrowful and touching. But he heard it, as if in a dream. His mind seemed wandering, and I was lulled into the most complete security. Never was indifference so well enacted—never had mortal been more attentive to a history than Harding to this. All its details had been carefully treasured up, and where the old lady had associated me with the adventures of her daughter, his mind had taken deep note, and the record in his memory was ineradicably written. Over the chimney place stood a rude portrait of the murdered girl, to which, when the old lady called for his attention to her beautiful features, he scarcely gave a glance; and he, whom destiny selected to bring the murderer of her child to punishment, provoked openly the anger of the mother, by his glaring inattention to the story of her supposed fate. We left the cottage after a somewhat protracted visit. I had no concern— not the slightest apprehension, so completely had my companion played his part in the transaction— but he had not lost a word, not a look not an action, in all the events of that morning. His eye was forever upon me—his thoughts were dissecting mine, and the most distant association of cause and effect, drawn vividly together by his intellect, quickened into sleepless exercise and energy by the influences acting upon it, supplied him with the materials for commencing the true history of my crime.

We passed the rock on our return. I could not keep my eyes from it; and his eyes were on mine. He saw the same ashy paleness of my cheek and look, and he saw that this rock had something to do with my history. In the analysis of a story like mine—so terribly romantic as it was—his imagination became a prime auxiliar, and with its aid, where a dull man would have paused for fact, with the felicity of truth, it supplied them, and he grew confident and strong in each hour of progression in his labor.

CHAPTER XV.

A week from this had not gone by, when, while under the hands of our village hair–dresser, I beheld a picture crowded among the hundred upon his walls, which filled me with astonishment, and awakened in my mind some moving apprehensions. I beheld the scene of my crime truly done to nature, and just by the little copse upon which the deed had been committed, stood a female form, pale and shadowy, and with a sufficient resemblance to Emily, to have been considered a portrait. You may guess my emotion. Having recovered from the first shock, I inquired, as if without the desire for an answer, where he got and who had painted it, and was told in reply that an old lady had brought it there for sale—the lady was unknown. Finding the price low—merely nominal, indeed, he had readily bought it; relying on the merits of the piece to insure it a ready sale. I affected to be pleased with it and paid him his price. Having secured it in possession, I examined it closely, and was confirmed in the opinion that the whole was copied from events in my own history. Beyond this I could perceive nothing farther. The preparation of the piece was a mystery, and I had not the courage to seek its developement. I cut up the tell–tale fabric with my knife, and witnessed its destruction, fragment by fragment, in the flames. Fool that I was, I did not dream that the artist had yet other copies. And so it was—another and another, to the number of three, appeared in the crowded shop of the hair–dresser. I was too sagacious, however, to purchase any more. I had begun to tremble! Still I had not the slightest suspicion of the author, and though my thoughts were restlessly employed upon the subject, they wandered to all persons and conjectured all things but the right. Still, daily, did Harding and myself pursue our rambles, and, each day, through his adroit ingenuity, yielded something more to the stock of that evidence which was to overwhelm me. By degrees, he had penetrated in all directions of that fatal wood; and, at length, our footsteps were bent, as in the most casual manner, up the steep sides of the rock, and over the very path, which, burdened with the dead body of Emily Andrews, I had once journeyed alone. My eyes were again riveted upon that fearful chasm—I heard the dead fall of her delicate form, as it struck from side to side in its passage down—I heard the clattering of the loosened stones which had accompanied and followed her; and, at length, the same subtle imagination which had revived all the circumstances vividly before one sense, arrayed her reanimated form as vividly before another. I saw her arise from the chasm, pale and ghastly as when I had seen her descend. For a moment the spell of terror fixed every faculty, and in that moment, the searching glance of my companion, had gathered much towards the formation of his testimony. He had followed the direction of my glance, and the chasm, half concealed in the umbrage, and not very obvious to the gaze, grew distinctly before him. I recovered from the trance which had for a time stupified me, and we returned to the village. In a few days more, and another scene, to me full of fearful meaning was in the shop of my hair–dresser. There was the rock—there the chasm, and just above, in a dim haze that made vague the expression and outline, but did not impair the features, stood the phantom person of Emily, as my imagination had borne it to my sight but a few days before. Who was it, that, with so much felicity, could embody my imaginings. I was thunderstruck, and, through the means of an agent, I secured this new accuser, and destroyed it in like manner with the former. But another self made its appearance, and, in despair, I gave up the hope of arresting, in this way, the progress of that inquiry, which, taking so equivocal a form, and pursuing a course so mysterious, was doubly terrible. But Harding, for he was the artist, did not alone content himself with probing the secrets of my soul, by exercising my fears and fancies. He privately took his way to the family of the murdered girl. He ascertained the day and date of her absence—he took careful note of our association—of the expectations that had been formed in their minds, not less than in the mind of Emily herself, from the attentions I had paid her; and though the true nature of our connexion had been totally unsuspected by the parents, our intimacy had been such as to warrant a belief, that, in the progress of events, something must necessarily grow out of it. He found that we had been almost in the daily habit of meeting, and in the very wood in which he had first perceived my terrors. He learned, that, in dragging the stream in its neighborhood, no traces had been found of the victim—that a search, made shortly after she had been missing, and on the same day, throughout the country, for many miles, had been ineffectual. He was conscious that few places of concealment offered themselves in the circuit so examined, except in the cavity of rock to which his mind had already adverted; and, associating the ill disguised apprehension and horror which I had exhibited while upon it, he came to the rapid conclusion that the mystery was to be developed there. Yet how was he now to proceed? There was still something wanting to unite together the several links in the chain of testimony which he had so assiduously and singularly woven. The circumstances, though strong, were not at all conclusive against me; and, having succeeded so poorly in the first instance, and with the public prejudice so strongly against him, he might well dread the overthrow of his design, in the event of any premature and partial development. Though perfectly satisfied that the chasm contained the remains of the murdered girl, he was yet well convinced how little the mere development of the body would avail, unless with some identifying circumstance, fixing the crime upon me. Accordingly, he devoted himself busily to the task of tracing in the details of the mother, all the particulars of my intimacy with the daughter. In this scrutiny he happened upon, read carefully, and copied a single note having my initials, merely, but without date, which I had sent her, enclosing some ornaments for her person and engaging to meet her on some day in the ensuing week. The style of expression was guarded in the extreme, and indicated the feelings of one who esteemed the individual he addressed, with a respectful consideration, which though not love itself, might in time, become so. The absence of a date, alone, presented a difficulty, which was only overcome, by a single passage which the note contained. It spoke of pressing engagements for a term of some weeks which would so occupy the attention of the writer as to leave him no opportunity of seeing her for that period unless that which the note suggested was embraced. What engagements were there of so pressing a character upon me? Harding knew as well as myself the nature of my employments, and felt assured that the assertion was either false, or that the note had been written at the time, when my marriage arrangements had been made; the only circumstance he conceived likely to have been looked to in my mind, as calculated to interfere with the pursuit of any humbler object. This was conjectural, however, yet the conjecture furnished him with an additional clue which he suffered not to escape him. The old lady could say nothing as to the period when the note had been received— but the jewels were shown him, and carefully noting down their kinds and qualities, he proceeded to the several shops of our village in which such articles were sold. He inspected all of corresponding description, and submitting those in question, he at length found out to whom and when they were sold. The dates were supplied, and were so far found to correspond with events, that it was indubitable that but four days after their purchase by myself, Emily Andrews had been lost to her family. The circumstances were now almost embodied in the estimation of the law; and assured, but still unprecipitate, Harding prepared calmly and quietly the whole narrative, and awaited impatiently the operation of looked for events, to unfold the entire history. And the time came!

CHAPTER XVI.

Fate had me in its power, and I was blind. If I were not weak enough, of myself, to reveal the secrets of my soul, and its crimes, I was not less the creature of a destiny, which, in the end, set at nought my profoundest cunning, and proved my wisdom to be the arrantest folly. I look back now with wonder at my own stupidity. A single survey into existing things, as in all other concerns I had certainly made it, and I should have laughed all inquisition to scorn. Now, I am its victim—the shallow victim of a most shallow design. Thus it is, however, that the wisest suffer defeat through a self–esteem which leads them into wrong, not merely in their estimate of themselves, but in their estimate of others. Thus was it with me; and well, from my own experience, may I exclaim with the ancient, " *fata viam invenient.* '

Yet was I not unwarned—unthreatened. I had a presentiment that something was to happen— I was uneasy, discontented—wandering. My spirits were dreadfully depressed, and but half conscious, I took my way to the secluded cottage of Harding. Unannounced, I entered his study, and found him—on his knees, at prayer. A strange feeling possessed me, and I was almost tempted to kneel down beside him. But I dared not—I had never been taught to worship—I had never been taught to bend the knee, and tones of supplication were foreign to my sense and unfamiliar to my lips. Could I have knelt at that moment and fervently prayed for the grace I had not, I feel satisfied the heart of my companion would have relented of all its purposes. He would not, at that moment, have arrested the new–born exercises of a spirit so redeeming and atoning. The moment of indulgence was permitted to escape, and the fiat had gone forth. The doom was upon me!

We sallied forth, as had been, for so long a period, our morning custom. A grave solemnity marked the expression of Harding's countenance, mixed, at intervals, as we grew more and more communicative, with a faltering hesitation of manner, indicating a relaxing of purpose. I can now comprehend all his feelings and emotions. His position was, indeed, a strange and sad one. Under a sense of duty the most sacred, not merely to the community, but to himself, he had undertaken the punishment of a criminal with whom he was in the daily habit of close communion—to whom, in worldly matters, he was somewhat indebted, and in whose welfare, he had at heart, and sincerely, a deep interest. The task of hypocrisy which he assumed, sufficiently painful to a mind like his, was doubly irksome under the operation of such circumstances; and, I am assured that could he, at that moment, have been persuaded of a change of heart in me—had I given him the slightest reason to believe that my crimes were regretted, and that it was my fixed purpose to become a better man,—he would, even then, just as the curtain was about to be drawn, which would unveil the whole catastrophe, have stayed his uplifted hand—he would have rather suffered the tortures of his imagination, and the rebukes of his ambition, than have cut off the penitent in his first approaches to pardon and atonement. But, at this moment, I uttered some vile jest—discreditable to manhood and morality, alike—and the spell was broken. He was strengthened in his purpose, and solemnly he led the way, I following, unconsciously, to my own sacrifice.

A sudden turn brought us directly upon the scene of my crime, and there, to my surprise, a goodly company were assembled.

"What is this!" was my exclamation. "Why are so many of the villagers here. Know you what is meant by this assemblage?"

"We shall see!" was his somewhat sudden and stern reply, as we continued to approach. My heart trembled, and leapt convulsively to my mouth—my knees faltered, but there was no retreat. We came up to the company before whom my appearance had scarcely been made, when, wildly from the group, rushed forth the mother of Emily—she seized me by my arm.

"Give me back my daughter" was her frenzied exclamation—"you will not keep her from me. My daughter—my poor sweet Emily."

They dragged her back to the spot, where, feebly and with an expression of subdued idiocy, old Andrews incessantly shook his stick in the direction where I stood, while his palsied head maintained a corresponding motion. I recovered myself, but my tones were husky and thick, and I am satisfied not so coherent as I could have wished them.

"What does all this mean, my friends; why this charge upon me—why this gathering—" was my inquiry.

"This gentleman will explain" said the Justice, pointing to Harding who had by this time taken a place midway between the company and myself, "you are charged, "continued the officer, "with having first seduced, then spirited away the daughter of these old people, one Emily Andrews; and for your sake, Mr. Faber, I sincerely hope that you may be able to establish your innocence in spite of the strong circumstances which will be brought against you."

I looked to Harding—I sought to crush him with that look—but he was untroubled, unappalled beneath it; and, though trembling with emotion, as seemingly determined in intention, as the martyr, fortifying if not establishing his faith, by the free offering of his blood. He proceeded, modestly, but confidently to his narration. He recounted the history of our intimacy—described once more the circumstances of the revelation which I had made, in his ears, of my crime. How it had burned in his heart like so many living coals. How he had come in his agony to me, and how finally, in order to escape from the suggestions of torture inflicted by conscience and imagination, he had revealed it as it had before been heard, to the officers of justice. He showed how he had been overthrown by the search made in accordance with the story— how, writhing under the reproaches of the public and crushed in their opinion, he had been on the verge of madness and suicide— how I had sought him out in his closet—repeated my story, and how he had again believed it. A certain something, he said, assured him that I had told the truth, but not the whole truth—that I had suppressed and altered, so as to defeat inquiry; but that, though the causes which had led me to disclose so much unnecessarily, were unknown and unaccountable, he was taught to believe in the commission of the crime. A desire to regain his station in society—to show that nothing of malice had prompted him in the first instance, inspired him with the design, which, carried out perseveringly and properly, had resulted in his being able, he thought, most satisfactorily to prove the murder of Emily Andrews by Martin Faber, and accordingly, he proceeded to the development of his particulars. How did I wonder at my own blindness as he proceeded in his narration. How did I wonder at the ingenuity with which, without any clue, he had unravelled, as with my own fingers, all my secret. He had watched all my motions— all my looks—all my words. He had suffered not a glance—not a whisper to escape him. With the assistance of his mother, who, herself, in disguise had sold them to the barber, he had carried on the affair of the pictures— he discovered who had bought them, and conjecturing for what purpose, he defied me to produce them. He described the involuntary terrors which my face had exhibited on approaching the spot upon which we stood— how the same emotion, so exhibited, had led him to suspect that the rock to which he pointed had also some connexion with the transaction. The facts gathered from the conversations with the family, leading to the final, and, as he thought, conclusive proof, in reference to the jewelry he next dwelt upon; and, with a brief but compact summary, he so concentrated the evidence, that, though strictly speaking, still inconclusive, there was not an individual present but was persuaded of my guilt.

"And now," said he, "there is but one more witness for examination, and this is the rock of which I have spoken. I am persuaded that the body of Emily Andrews lies there. The expression of Faber's eye—the whole look with which he surveyed the chasm, could not have come from nothing. That rock, in some way or other, is associated with his crime. I have made arrangements for its examination and we shall soon judge."

Placing a little ivory whistle to his lips, a shrill sound went through the forest, and after the lapse of a moment, a sudden flash illuminated, and a loud explosion shook the earth around us. We proceeded to the spot, and when the smoke had cleared away, a shout from those who traversed the fragments, torn from the fissure which had been split by gun–powder, announced the discovery of the victim, and in her hands—conclusive evidence against me—torn from my bosom without my knowledge, while in the last convulsion of death,—lay the large brooch, the loss of which had given me so much concern at the time, and, on its back, chased finely in the gold setting, were the initials of my name.

CHAPTER XVII.

He came to me in my dungeon—he, my accuser—my enemy—my friend. In the first emotions of my wrath, I would have strangled him, and I shook my chains in his face, and I muttered savage curses and deep threats in his ears. He stood patiently and unmoved. His hands were clasped, and his eyes were dim, and for a while he had no language, no articulations.

"Think not," at last he spoke—"think not I have come to this work with a feeling of satisfaction. I have suffered more agony in its progress than I can well describe or you understand— I will not attempt it. If you cannot, from what you know of my character, conceive the grief and sickness of heart which must have come over me, during the long period and regular and frequent succession of hours, in which I was required to play the hypocrite—I cannot teach it you. I come not for this. I come to ask your forgiveness—to implore your better opinion—and that you may attribute to a necessity which gave me no other alternatives than death or shame, the whole of this painful episode in my life!

He was a noble creature, and so I could not but think at that very moment; but, I was of the earth, earthy! I was a thing of comprehensive malignity, and my impulses were perpetually warring with the suggestions of my sense.

"My death be upon your head—my ignominy be yours—the curses of all of mine be on you—may all things curse you. Talk of my being a murderer, are you less so? Have you not hurried me to death—a shameful death—dishonoring myself, dishonoring my family, when I might have atoned for the error of my youth, in the progress and better

48

performances of my age? Hypocrite, that you are, begone! Come not falsely now to extenuate what you may not excuse—your priestly cant about forgiveness does not deceive me. Away—I curse you to the last!"— and his head sunk upon his breast, and his hands were clasped in agony, and I exulted in the writhing and gnawing of that heart, whose over–delicate structure, I well knew, could never sustain such reproaches.

"Spare me, spare me! As I live you do me wrong. Be not so merciless—so unforgiving. Fame, and the world's good opinion, were to me the breath of life. I could not have done other than I did and lived—I could not."

"Looked you then to me to do it? Was the world's good opinion nothing to me? Had I nothing to live for? Had I no aim in life? Oh—away! I sicken but to see you!"

Patiently, amidst all my reproaches, he persisted in the endeavour to conciliate my fiendish mood, suggesting a thousand excuses and reasons, for the obvious duty which I myself felt he had done to himself and to society— but I rejected them all, and, in despair, he was about to retire, when a sudden thought came over me.

"Stay, Harding—there is one thing—there is one way in which I can be assured that your motive was not malicious, and that you have been stimulated as you say, solely by a belief in the necessity of what you have done!"

"Speak—say, any thing, but grant me your forgiveness—give me your good opinion!"

"Ridiculous! the good opinion of a murderer— the hated, the despised of the community;— of what good is it to you or to any body?"

"True—true!—but even with the murderer I would be at peace—I would not have him die with an ill feeling towards me. But there is yet another thought which prompts the desire in his case. It is from my associate and companion that I would have forgiveness, for the violation of that confidence which grew out of that association. For this I would have your forgiveness!"

"The distinction is somewhat nice, but you shall have what you ask—cheerfully have it— upon one condition!"

"What is that, say on—I will gladly serve you."

"Justice demands a victim and I must die; but it is not necessary to justice that I should die in a particular manner. I would not die by the rope, in the presence of a gaping multitude— you must provide me with a dagger— a knife, any thing by which I may free myself from the ignominy of such a death."

"Impossible! that will be wrong—it will be criminal. Justice, it is true, may not care whether the rope or the steel shall serve her purposes, but she requires that her officer, at least, shall do it; otherwise it is not her act. It is your will, not hers, that would be performed— her claim would be defeated."

"Shallow sophistry!—this then is your friendship—but I knew it would be so— away, and may—"

He stopped me in my curse.—

"Stay!"—he exclaimed hurriedly, and with terror—"any thing but that. I will do as you require."

CHAPTER XVIII.

The day of retribution—of a fearful trial, is come!—Horrible mockery!—the sunlight streams through the iron grating, and falls upon the straw of this accursed dungeon. How beautifully—how wooingly it looks—lovelier than ever, about to be forever lost! Do I tremble— would I yet live and linger out the years in a life of curses, among those who howl their denunciations forever in my ears? Could I survive this exposure, this infamy, and cherish life on any terms and at all hazards! I would not die—not thus, not thus—on that horrible scaffolding, I shudder but to think on. Yet what hope would I rely upon? I have none to whom in this perilous hour, I would turn in expectation. No fond spirit now labors, unsleepingly, for my relief. I have not lived for such an interest—I have not sought to enlist such affections—none hope—none seek my escape—none would assist in its consummation! I am alone—I must die!— and what,—horrible thought!—if he should not bring the weapon?—if his shrinking and woman–like conscience should scruple, thus, to interfere with the decree of justice, and I should be led out in the accursed cart, through the jeering multitude, and go through all the trials of that death of shame and muscular agony!—let me not think of it. Let me not think!—

And I closed my eyes as if to shut out thought, and rushed to the extremest corner of my cell, despairing of the appearance of Harding with the dagger he had promised. But a few hours were left, and the sharp and repeated strokes of the hammer, at a little distance, indicated the rapid progress of the executioner in his preparations for the terrible performance of his office. I groaned in my agony of thought, and buried my head still deeper in the meshes of my couch.—Thanks, thanks—the fates be praised—he comes—the bolts shoot back—the doors are unbarred—he is here! I live again—I shall not stand then on that fearful fabric. He brings me that which shall enable me to give it my defiance, and disappoint the gaping multitude, already beginning to assemble. I shall defeat them still!

"Oh, Harding—I had almost given you up— I had begun to despond—to despair. I dreaded that the weakness of your spirit had yielded to your conscience, and that you had forgotten your pledge. God of terror! what a horrible agony the thought brought along with it. It is well you came; I had else cursed you with spectres that would have fastened on you like wolves. They would have drained the blood, at the same moment, from all the arteries in your system. Give me the knife."

"It is here, and, oh, Martin—I have had a terrible struggle with my own sense of what is right in the performance of this office. I have resisted the suggestions of conscience— I have overcome the rebukes of my own mind— I have done wrong, and do not seek to excuse myself—but I have brought you what you desired. Here, take it, take it at once and quickly before I repent me of having so weakly yielded in the struggle."

"I have it—I have it!" I shouted wildly— shaking the naked blade as if in defiance, in the direction of the scaffold. "I am secure from that shame—I shall not be the capped and culprit thing of ignominy which they would make me, in the eyes of that morbid rabble. I am free from the dishonor of such a death. Ah, Harding, thou hast almost redeemed thy fault—thou hast almost taught me to forgive thee for thy offending. Nay—I could almost forbear to howl my curses in thy ears, and avoid saying to thee, as I do—may the furies tug at thy vitals, like snakes, in all hours—"

"Forbear, forbear!" he shrieked—oh, cruel; wantonly cruel as thou art—where is thy promise, Martin—where is thy honor—wilt thou deceive me?"

"Ha! ha! ha!—fool that thou art—didst thou not deceive and betray me? Where was thy honor, false hypocrite—where was thy forbearing mercy? Wert thou not cruel, wantonly cruel then? Hell's curses be upon thee—I would have thee live forever to enjoy them—thou shouldst have an eternity of torment— thou shouldst have an exaggerated sense of life for its better appreciation. Forbearance, indeed! No—I would invent a curse for thee that—and ha! thou art come in season, at the fit moment, to be my help in imprecation. Come forward—thou has lips would make an oath tell—and tell to the quick. Come hither, come hither, my Constance!"

And he dragged forward the young and terrified wife, who had just then made her appearance in the dungeon, and forcing her upon her knees before him, he stood over her, waving the gleaming dagger in her eyes.

"Thou shalt kneel, Constance!—it is a solemn moment, and thou hast that to perform which requires that word and action should well suit its solemnity. Ay, fold thy hands upon thy breast—yet I ask thee not to pray— thou must curse and not pray. Speak then as I tell thee—speak and palter with me not, for, doomed as I am to death, and hopeless of escape, as I have nothing now to hope, I have nothing now to apprehend from man. Speak after me, then, as thou hast a love for life—as thou hast a leading and a lasting terror of a horrible death!"

Agonized with the situation of Constance, Harding advanced to interfere, but with a giant–like strength, the criminal hurled him back with a single arm, while he threatened, if he again approached, to bury the weapon in the bosom of the kneeling and terror–stricken woman. On a sudden, she recovered her energies, and in coherent but feeble tones, she called upon her husband to proceed.

"It is well thou art thus docile. Thou art wise, Constance—thou art obedient, as thou hast ever been. Keep thy hands folded, and speak after me—say, in thy wonted manner to thy God—bid him hearken to thy prayer—bid him, in tenderness and love for thee, to grant it as thou makest it. Promise him largely of thy increased love and obedience for this. Promise him thy exclusive devotion—say thou wilt live only for him; and strive to forget all the other attractions, whatever they may be, of life and society. I care not if thou keepest these pledges, it is enough for me that thou makest them."

She did as she was required. She implored the Father, fervently to sanction the prayer she was about to make—she vowed her whole love and duty, in return, so far as her poor capacities would permit, entirely to him. She spoke in the fullnecs of accumulated feelings, and with a devotion as deep and touching, as it was tearless and dignified.

"Well—that is enough. Thou hast been as liberal in promises, as I could well desire thee; and now for the prayer and petition thou hast to offer. Look on this man—the murderer of thy husband—the wretch, who, wouldst thou believe it, my Constance, has the audacity to have a love even for thee, in his cruel heart—the wretch, whom—thou wilt be slow to think so, my Constance, but it is true—whom thou dost love—"

She looked up to him, as he proceeded, with a most imploring expression—but he had no touch of pity in his soul. He proceeded—

"It is true, and you dare not deny it, my Constance. You love the wretch who has murdered your husband, and, perhaps, when my bloody grave, which his hands have dug, has been well covered over, you will take shelter in his bosom—"

The wretched woman shrieked in agony, and fell at length upon the floor—but he allowed her no respite. After a few moments, making her resume her position upon her knees, he continued—

"Him, thou must curse! Say after me— God of heaven and earth, if thou be, as thou art said to be, just in thy provisions— Say on!"

She repeated: He went on.—

"If the power be in thee, as I believe, to do the will of thy creatures on earth—"

She repeated.

"If thou canst curse and bless—build up and destroy—yield pleasure or pain—make happy or miserable—"

She repeated.

"I call upon thee, with thy agents and ministering powers to curse with thy eternal wrath—to blister with thy unceasing severities—to torture with thy utmost varieties of pain—to make sore the body—to make bitter the life—to make wretched the spirit—to pursue at all seasons and in all lands, with thy unceasing and most aggravated asperities, this bloody man, the destroyer of my husband."

The youth, upon whom this imprecation was to fall, rushed forward—

"Speak it not! oh, speak it not, lady!—in charity speak it not. I can bear with the curse from his lips—from any lips—but thine. Sanction not, I pray you, this wantoness of cruelty—pardon rather, and forgive me that I have been the unwilling, and, in all times, the sad instrument of Providence in this proceeding."

"Back, back, William Harding—the curse must be uttered—it must be felt—it must be borne. Speak on, Constance Faber—speak on—as I have told it thee. She looked up in his face with the calm resignation of a saint— and, as one entering upon the pilgrimage of martyrdom, she proceeded regularly in the formula, sentence after sentence, which he had prescribed; while he, standing above, muttered his gratification as every added word seemed to arouse new agonies in the bosom of the denounced. But, as she reached the part assigned to the application of the curse, she entreated these curses upon the head of Constance Faber, if she should ever teach her lips to invoke other than blessings upon any being of the human family, whatever, in the sight of heaven or of earth, his offence might be! The glare from the eyes of the disappointed criminal was that of a hyena, robbed of his prey. A malignant shriek burst from his lips, as, with uplifted arm and furious stroke, he aimed the weapon at her bosom. Harding sprang forward, but the weapon, as she swooned away from the blow, had penetrated her side. The youth, with unlooked for power, tore her from his grasp, before his blow could be repeated, and bore her out of his reach to the opposite part of the cell. The keeper and his assistants rushed in upon the prisoner. As they approached, he aimed the bloody dagger at his own bosom, but, at that instant, fear came over his heart—the fates had paralyzed him—he was a coward! he shrunk back from the stroke and the dagger fell from his hands. Without difficulty he was in a moment secured. Constance was but slightly wounded, yet happily, enough so, to be entirely ignorant of the horrors of the scene so malignantly forced upon her. In his cell, the wretch howled over the unperforming weakness of his hand, which had not only

54

failed to secure him his victim, but had left him without the ability to defeat his doom.

* * * * * * *

The hour is come! O cursed weakness, that I should fail at that moment of escape—But the fates had written it—I must fulfil my destiny. My eyes grow dim—I fail to see any longer the crowd—all is confused and terrible. What spectres are these that surround me? It is Emily,—and why does the old father shake his palsied hand in my face—will no one keep off the intruders?—they have no concern here. I have raved—but now all is before me. What a multitude—does this suffering of a fellow creature give them pleasure! Should I ask—I who have lived in that enjoyment! Would I had also been weak; I should have escaped this exposure— this pain. It is but for a moment, however— but a momentary thrill; and then—fate will have no secrets. I shall no longer be its blind victim—its slave. There is an old man at the foot of the scaffold, that I would not see there! It is old Andrews. Would he were gone—or that I could look elsewhere. But no matter—it will soon be over. I would I had a God at this moment—better to have believed— on earth there is nothing for me—such a faith, though folly, had been grateful. But now—now it is too late. The hour is come!— The sunlight and the skies are gone—gone— gone—gone."

CPSIA information can be obtained
at www.ICGtesting.com
Printed in the USA
BVHW060311090821
613824BV00003B/83